GUNHAND FROM TEXAS

Center Point
Large Print

Also by William Heuman and available from Center Point Large Print:

Heller from Texas
Guns at Broken Bow
On to Santa Fe
Then Came Mulvane

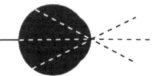

GUNHAND FROM TEXAS

William Heuman

CENTER POINT LARGE PRINT
THORNDIKE, MAINE

This Center Point Large Print edition
is published in the year 2021 by arrangement with
Golden West Literary Agency.

Originally published in the US by Avon Books.

The text of this Large Print edition is unabridged.
In other aspects, this book may vary
from the original edition.
Printed in the United States of America
on permanent paper.
Set in 16-point Times New Roman type.

ISBN: 978-1-63808-087-9 (hardcover)
ISBN: 978-1-63808-091-6 (paperback)

The Library of Congress has cataloged this record
under Library of Congress Control Number: 2021940851

GUNHAND
FROM
TEXAS

CHAPTER 1

Standing out in front of the Elkhorn National Bank, unshaven, his black hair beginning to curl at his neck, his clothing about as badly worn as that of any of the trail riders who'd come up with him from Texas, Emmett Kane definitely did not look like a man who had a bank draft for twelve thousand dollars in his shirt pocket.

He stood there for a few moments, relishing this suddenly acquired freedom, and the small fortune in his pocket. For over four months, day and night, in heat and cold, in storm and calm, he'd played nursemaid to thirty-five hundred tough Texas steers, stock he'd purchased from Texas cattlemen on the Brazos bottoms and driven up the long, long trail to Wyoming.

The stock had been turned over to the buyer yesterday, and all through the day the count had been made. Early this morning Emmett had ridden into Elkhorn with the buyer, after paying off his dozen riders. Two minutes before, after having the draft drawn up inside the bank, the buyer had shaken hands with Emmett, stepped into his buckboard, and driven off.

The buyer was gone; the thirty-five-hundred-odd head of stock had been driven off to a distant Wyoming range. Emmett's trail riders were gone,

7

having taken the early morning train to Omaha, where they could let off some of the steam which had been building up inside them the final few weeks of the drive. Elkhorn didn't offer sufficient entertainment for men who for a whole summer had looked at nothing but Texas steers and each other, and had become heartily sick of both.

Emmett took a deep breath, put one shoulder against the upright supporting the wooden awning which stretched out to the edge of the walk, and then started to roll a cigarette. He didn't know whether it was the newfound freedom, or the bracing October atmosphere of this north country which affected him most, but he felt lighthearted, and he wondered if this were the normal experience of a Texas man new to the north country.

He had much to do this morning. He needed a shave and a haircut, and a bath, and he had to throw out all his clothing and purchase an entirely new outfit. He had his riding horse and his saddle stabled in the Emerald Corral around the corner, and he had to sell them before he took the train to Omaha, and then back to Texas—if he returned to Texas. For the first time since the previous winter, when he'd been buying up stock for the long drive north, he had no plans, and nothing particular to do—and it felt good.

A lone rider pulled up in front of the tie-rack before the bank, dismounted, swinging the reins around the bar, and then ducked under the bar and came toward Emmett on the board walk.

Emmett had been looking down at the cigarette he'd started to roll. When he lifted his eyes, aware that the rider had paused in front of him, he stared with some surprise into the blue-gray eyes of a tall, rather slender girl with copper-colored hair under her black, flat-crowned hat.

She had stopped in front of him, and for the first time Emmett became aware of his appearance. He wished he'd taken time out this morning for at least a shave and a haircut, but the whole affair had been so rushed, the buyer so anxious to start north with his stock, there had been little time for anything but business.

She wasn't a particularly beautiful girl. Her face was tanned, and she had a rather wide mouth. Her nose was straight, and there were some freckles around it. When she spoke her voice was low, almost hard. She said quietly, "Are you a Texan?"

Emmett Kane touched his hat. He said, "Yes, ma'am." There had undoubtedly been many Texans in Elkhorn this summer, because four other cattle drives had been made from the Lone Star State into Wyoming. He realized that he looked the part of a Texas trail driver in his worn Levi's, down-at-the-heels boots, the torn, scuffed leather jacket.

"I'm Madge Wilson," the girl said. "I run Pine Tree up in Vermilion Valley. If you're looking for work, ride out this afternoon. I'm taking on riders."

"Yes, ma'am," Emmett nodded. He didn't smile, even though it was a humorous situation. He had sufficient money in his shirt pocket to start a ranch of his own, and possibly a bigger one than this girl owned, but she had mistaken him for a trail rider with a month's wages in his pockets, ready to blow it in as soon as the sun went down.

"If you have any friends," Miss Wilson went on in that same low, hard voice, "you can bring them along with you."

Emmett put the cigarette into his mouth, but didn't light it. He said thoughtfully, "Reckon you're planning on a pretty busy winter, ma'am." Even as he said this he realized it was an anomaly. The fall roundup was over, and ordinarily the local ranchers would be dropping men rather than hiring them.

"We're anticipating a busy winter," the tall girl said with a mirthless smile. "Ride out, if you're a man who likes action."

She nodded to him, and went on into the bank. Emmett put a match to the cigarette, got it going, and then started across the street toward the barber shop. As he went around the tie-rack he had a look at the sorrel horse Madge Wilson had ridden. It was a good animal, short and stocky, with the heavy coat characteristic of these northern mounts. He'd heard that they needed the heavy coats for the terrific winters they had in Wyoming. The Pine Tree brand was stamped on the left hip of the sorrel horse.

Coming up on the walk across the street, Emmett turned left in the direction of the barber shop, which was three doors beyond the Cattleman's Saloon. A thin-faced, blunt-nosed young fellow with ash-blond hair stood out in front of the saloon, hands hooked in his gunbelt, a cigarette in his mouth.

As Emmett moved past him, unhurriedly, the rider said casually, "Don't do it, Texas."

Emmett stopped walking. He turned around slowly, a curious, half-humorous expression in his gray eyes. He said, "Don't do what?"

"Don't ride out to Vermilion Valley," the other told him evenly.

Emmett put his hands in his back pockets as he spread his legs on the walk, facing the man directly now. He said thoughtfully, "No?"

"No," the rider said flatly.

Emmett tilted the cigarette upward in his mouth. He was smiling, still apparently in good humor, but his gray eyes were a shade lighter in color.

"Why not?" he asked.

"You'll find out, if you head out that way."

He pushed away from the wall of the building, then, moving past Emmett, and as he did so he deliberately thrust against Emmett with his right shoulder. It wasn't a hard thrust, and it didn't move Emmett from his position on the walk. It was intended to give a little extra emphasis to the warning he'd just delivered, and as such Emmett Kane did not like it.

As the blunt-nosed fellow went by, Emmett put out his right hand, resting it on the rider's shoulder, turning him around gently but firmly. His voice was soft, deliberate, as he spoke.

"Plenty of room on this walk, Jack."

"Take your hand off me!" the rider snapped; then, before Emmett could do it, he reached up and slapped the restraining hand from his shoulder. He lashed out hard, and Emmett, who would have been willing to let the incident ride, came back at him instantly, grasping him by the shirt with his right hand and ramming him back against the wall of the building, shaking him up considerably.

The rider let out a short yelp of surprised alarm, and struggled to regain his footing. He had hard, pale blue eyes which had been very sure before— but there was some uncertainty in them now.

Emmett stepped back suddenly, standing about five feet away on the walk. He said softly, "There's a beginning to it, Jack. You want to take it up from there?"

Both men wore guns, the blunt-nosed rider a Smith & Wesson .44 in a smooth black holster. Emmett wore the Colt .45 he'd carried all the way from Texas. He didn't think it would come to gunfire, and looking into the other's eyes he learned that it wouldn't come to fists, either.

Emmett watched him for a moment, seeing the truculence die out of him, and then he relaxed, a small smile playing around the corners of his mouth.

"Maybe," Emmett told him quietly, "you'd better move along now, Jack."

The moment of danger was over, and the rider sensed it. He was all bluster and pride again as he stepped away from the wall. He said grimly, "You better remember what I told you, mister."

Emmett just smiled at him, recognizing this threat for what it was—a sop to his blasted vanity. He didn't say anything, and the man strode off the walk to a big bay horse at the tie-rack. He mounted and rode away, jerking the animal's mouth with unnecessary violence.

Emmett glanced at the brand mechanically. It was a king's crown—a new brand to him. He went on toward the barber shop, where he found only one customer ahead of him.

When he finally sat down in the chair he said to the barber, "I'd like a bath after I finish up here."

"I'll heat the water," the barber told him, and he went to the rear of the shop. When he came back and started to work on Emmett's long hair he said jocularly, "Reckon they keep pretty warm down in Texas with hair like this."

"Grows fast on the trail," Emmett murmured, "and no barbers from the Brazos to Elkhorn."

"Staying for the winter?" the barber asked him.

Emmett shrugged slightly. He had no plans, but he didn't particularly relish the thought of a cold Wyoming winter. In all his life he'd seen snow only once, and then only a few inches of it.

"You never saw the winters we have here," the barber boasted. "Three and four feet of snow on the flats—and cold! Keeps piling up one after the other."

"How does the stock weather it?" Emmett asked.

"Up till last winter," the barber explained, "ranchers around here just let 'em drift and fend for themselves. They learned to kick the snow and ice away from the bunchgrass, and they licked snow for water. Got by all right—till last winter, which was a tough one. Every rancher in Wyoming lost stock, and some of them a good part of their herd. They're scared stiff this winter."

"What can they do?" Emmett wanted to know.

"Most of 'em have been worrying themselves sick all summer trying to figure that out. They're scared now of another tough winter. A lot of them have been chasing all over Wyoming trying to find isolated valley ranges which they can rent, anything with one high wall on the north side to stop some of that snow piling in."

"Reckon there wouldn't be too many places like that," Emmett observed thoughtfully.

"Only one around Elkhorn," the barber explained, "is Vermilion Valley, Madge Wilson's place. Understand she didn't lose a head last winter—walls all around it, seven thousand feet high to the north. When we get two feet of snow in Elkhorn, she might get one foot, an' it's them twelve inches decide whether a steer toughs it out through the winter, or goes under."

Emmett thought about that as he studied his reflection in the shop mirror. It started to shape up now, why Miss Wilson was hiring riders to work her range during the fall and winter months, when other ranchers were dropping men. Texans had a reputation up this way for toughness and quickness with a sixgun, and very possibly Miss Wilson was concerned with threats or rumors that other ranchers would attempt to move into her valley.

Emmett said casually, "What outfit carries a crown brand in this country?"

"King's crown?" the barber said. "That'll be the big English outfit—Wyoming Land and Cattle Company, run by Mr. Clyde Morrison. Comes from London, England."

"Englishman?" Emmett murmured.

"Quite a few of them up this way," the barber explained. "You'll find more Crown cattle in these parts than all the other stock combined. Most of the Englishmen run their ranches from across the water, with a range boss in charge. Mr. Morrison is on the ground—a gentleman with blue blood in his veins, but from what I can see there's nobody in this part of the country pushing him around."

He nudged Emmett suddenly with his elbow

and said softly, "Talk of the devil! There he is—coming in to Elkhorn with Boyd Halloran, his range boss."

Emmett turned to look through the window. Two riders were moving by at a walk past the front of the shop. Emmett saw the Crown brands on the hips of both horses, a big black gelding with three white legs, and a chestnut.

Clyde Morrison rode the black, and Emmett didn't have to be told which man was the Englishman. Morrison rode a peculiar, low-cantled English saddle, the first one Emmett had ever seen. He wore a checked tweed riding coat and breeches, with English boots, and looking at him for the first time a man would be inclined to smile at the outfit.

Looking at his dark, somber face, however, with the solid, bulldog jaws, the blunt nose and the dark, beetling eyebrows, Emmett was inclined to believe, along with the barber, that not too many did smile at Morrison or his outfit. If they did, they didn't smile twice.

Halloran, the Crown range boss, was a different type entirely, a light-complexioned man with strawberry-blond hair, big, with wide shoulders and a thick waist. He had a big prow of a nose to go with his wide, smooth-shaven face, and he rode easily in the saddle, body swaying with the movements of the horse, where Morrison's carriage was stiffly erect.

The two riders passed out of sight, and Emmett settled himself in the barber's chair. He said to the barber, "This Wyoming Land and Cattle Company after Miss Wilson's Vermilion Valley?"

"Ain't a rancher around here," the barber chuckled, "wouldn't give his right arm for it just for winter range. But old Jed Wilson was in there first, and it's been Pine Tree range ever since. Jed passed on two years ago, and Miss Wilson's been running Pine Tree. Does a good job, too."

"Big outfit?" Emmett wanted to know.

"Small," the barber explained, "but it should have been the biggest in the state. Jed Wilson was the first rancher up here with a trailherd from Texas. If he'd had his girl's push and drive he'd have been as big as Crown is now."

"Takes drive," Emmett murmured.

He had his haircut and his shave, and he spent an hour in the galvanized bathtub in the rear of the shop. When he paid his bill and stepped out into the street again, he felt like a new man. He needed clothing, and the barber directed him to a shop a few doors beyond the hotel at the corner.

Stepping out of the shop, breathing in again this racy northern air, already tinged with the almost indefinable smell of snow, Emmett headed up toward the hotel. He walked west, the high peaks of the Elkhorn Range forming a backdrop for the town. Snow covered the tops of the highest peaks— the first snow he'd ever seen on mountains.

With each passing hour he was becoming more impressed with this north country. The people moved at a faster rate in the streets; they spoke more rapidly, and they seemed intent on getting things done. Already, the idea was forming in his mind that he would take his time about returning to Texas; that he would spend the winter here just to see the big snows of which he'd heard so much.

Out in front of the hotel he spotted Clyde Morrison's black gelding and Boyd Halloran's chestnut, and then he saw the two men standing on the porch, looking steadily in his direction as he approached. With them was the blunt-nosed Crown rider he'd met earlier in the morning.

Emmett Kane pursed his lips into a tuneless whistle as he moved leisurely toward the hotel. It was becoming quite apparent that he was already involved in the affairs of Elkhorn, whether he'd wanted to be or not.

CHAPTER 2

Boyd Halloran stepped off the porch, moving out to the edge of the walk, as Emmett approached. He had a fresh cigar in his mouth, and he stood with his heavy legs spread, hands hooked in his back pockets, watching Emmett approach.

Morrison, the Englishman, remained on the porch, facing Emmett, his back against one of the porch pillars, arms folded, that somber expression on his face.

The blunt-nosed rider with the blond hair sat on the top step of the porch, lips drawn back in a kind of sneer, eyes narrowed.

As Emmett came up, Halloran said easily, "That him, Lee?"

Lee nodded. "King of the walk," he said tersely, "like all them damn Texans."

Emmett slowed down, and then came to a full stop. He looked at Halloran, and then he looked at the rider, a faint, cool smile on his face. He said to the Crown rider, "Reckon you got yourself a little help, Lee. You figure you needed it?"

Lee muttered something under his breath, and hate was in his pale blue eyes.

Boyd Halloran said from the outer edge of the walk, "Staying in this part of the country, Texas?"

"Why?" Emmett asked him.

Halloran had turquoise-colored eyes, and a flicker of annoyance showed in them as he shifted the cigar from one side of his mouth to the other. Before he could speak, Lee spoke up again, irrepressible this noon, trying to redeem his pride. He said sourly, "They're all like that, Halloran. You show 'em black and they'll swear it's white. They're ornery."

Emmett rubbed his hands thoughtfully on his worn Levi's. He said softly, "You talk a lot, Lee."

"I'll talk—" the rider started hotly, but Boyd Halloran's voice came at him like a whip.

"Shut up, Ransom."

Morrison spoke from the porch in a clipped, precise way. "Are you looking for work?"

He addressed the remark to Emmett, who looked up at him coolly. Glancing first at Lee Ransom, and then at Halloran, Emmett said casually, "Not with this outfit."

Clyde Morrison's heavy jaws clamped shut. He had black eyes and heavy black eyebrows, and he looked older than Emmett fancied he was—a man in his early thirties, probably a few years older than himself.

"Your privilege," he said briefly.

Lee Ransom couldn't be restrained. "Like I said," he snarled from the top step of the porch, "you show 'em black, and—"

He didn't get any farther. Emmett suddenly stepped forward, reached out with his right hand

and grasped the Crown rider's left ankle. He yanked hard and Lee Ransom flew off the step, landing on the board walk on his back, his hat rolling from his head.

Emmett said to him softly, "You were told once to shut up, Ransom." He glanced at Boyd Halloran, wondering if the Crown range boss would come into it, and then he heard the quick steps on the walk, coming toward them.

Halloran hadn't moved from his position on the outer edge of the walk, and he'd turned his head slightly to see who was coming up. Ransom was scrambling to his feet, face white with rage, when Madge Wilson came up behind him, her blue eyes hard. She addressed herself to Halloran, assuming he was behind the altercation. She said bitterly, "You have your nerve, Halloran, molesting my riders right on the main street of Elkhorn."

She was not alone. Emmett noticed the tall, dark-haired young man behind her, coming up slowly, as if reluctant to become involved in the affair. He was good-looking, almost too handsome, with a well-shaped nose and mouth, brown eyes with long lashes, and long sideburns. Emmett guessed him to be about twenty-five.

There was no strength in his chin or his mouth, and the way he lingered behind Miss Wilson immediately formed Emmett's opinion of him. He was a man who would have a certain appeal for women, but not particularly for men. This opinion was strengthened by the half-contemptuous glance Boyd Halloran sent in his direction.

Halloran said coolly, "This chap ride for you, Miss Wilson?"

He'd taken the cigar from his mouth and touched his hat briefly as she addressed him.

Madge Wilson looked at Emmett, faint surprise coming into her eyes. She'd seen him earlier in the morning, unshaven, his hair very long, looking exactly what he'd appeared to be—a drifter in off one of the trailherds.

He was clean-shaven now and his hair was cut. He looked more his twenty-eight years, and his face had its redeeming features. His nose had a slight dent in the bridge, and there was a cleft in his chin, and his gray eyes were clear and steady. But his clothes were still disreputable, and he wished fervently that he'd stopped in the clothing store before getting his haircut and shave so that at this moment he could have looked more respectable.

Madge Wilson was saying tersely, "I've asked him to ride for Pine Tree."

It was a statement which could have been taken several ways. Emmett realized that she was trying to protect him by intimating that he was a Pine Tree rider, even though she knew he hadn't committed himself.

Halloran concluded that Emmett had signed with

Pine Tree, and he said carelessly, "Lee, here, just had a few words with him, Miss Wilson. Nothing to get excited about."

Emmett glanced up at the porch where Clyde Morrison was standing, and he was the only one in the group who happened to be looking that way. He surprised a peculiar expression on the Englishman's face. Morrison was looking straight at Madge Wilson, and for the moment that somber expression had left his heavy face. He was a man looking at a woman the way a woman liked to be looked at. He was a man who very well could be in love.

When Madge Wilson glanced at him, Emmett noticed that he was himself again, somber, unsmiling, a reserved man whose thoughts always were his own. Emmett was quite sure the owner of Pine Tree had no intimation that Clyde Morrison looked upon her in any other light than that of a rival rancher.

Lee Ransom was staring at Emmett out of feverish eyes, and Emmett told himself that in walking about this town at night he had better approach each dark alley with the greatest caution.

Boyd Halloran said to him, "All right, Ransom. Clear out."

The Crown rider turned on his heel and strode away, and Emmett saw him enter a saloon adjoining the hotel. Boyd Halloran nodded to Miss Wilson, gave Emmett a bland look, and then went up on the porch. He and Morrison went into the hotel.

Emmett touched his hat. He said to the girl, "I'm obliged, ma'am."

"You didn't need much help, from what I could see," Madge Wilson chuckled. "That offer still goes at Pine Tree, if you want to ride out."

"Think about it," Emmett told her. He glanced at the handsome man rolling a cigarette a few yards away, making no attempt to come forward and be introduced.

Moving on to the store the barber had recommended, Emmett stepped inside, found it empty, and made his purchases. He bought everything new—Levi's, several warm flannel shirts, boots, a hat, a leather jacket to take the place of the one he was wearing, and woolen socks.

He changed into the new clothes in the back room of the store, and when he came out to pay the bill he had on an entirely new outfit with the exception of the gunbelt.

He said to the shopkeeper, "Who's that rider passing now with Miss Wilson?"

"Dean Brockton," the man told him. "Owns Bar B at the mouth of Vermilion Valley. Neighbor of Madge Wilson's."

Emmett paid for the new clothing, which came to a considerable sum, and he still had the twelve-thousand-dollar draft in his pocket, which he could cash or deposit whenever he wished.

Before he left the shop, however, he had one more question to ask, and he told himself that he was a fool for going even that far. He said, "Where is Vermilion Valley?"

"Take the stage road north out of Elkhorn," the shopkeeper explained. "Follow it maybe four miles. You'll see the big Wyoming Land and Cattle Company spread on the left. Another mile and you hit a dirt road running west into the hills. Go over two hogbacks and you come to the entrance to the valley—prettiest place you ever saw. Little stream by the name of Squaw Run goes past the mouth of the valley. Another reason why Pine Tree and Bar B should unite."

"How's that?" Emmett asked.

"No water in the valley," the shopkeeper told him. "Everything else, but no water. Pine Tree has always had the use of Squaw Run on Bar B range. Tom Brockton and Jed Wilson had an agreement. Since both of them died, of course, the agreement still stands. Pine Tree stock waters on Bar B land."

Emmett considered that. "Brockton and Miss Wilson get along, I suppose," he said.

"Getting married, I hear," the shopkeeper grinned. "There'll be no fighting about water rights there."

"That's so," Emmett nodded.

Putting on his new hat, he stepped out into the street, ravenously hungry now as it was past one o'clock in the afternoon.

He remembered that the hotel had a dining room, and he retraced his steps, entering the dining room from the street entrance rather than going in through the lobby. He was sitting down at a corner table when he saw Clyde Morrison, Halloran, and another man, sitting at a table on the other side of the room.

Both Morrison and Halloran had seen him come through the door, and they'd looked at him curiously. The clothes had considerably transformed him; he looked less like a drifter and more like a fairly prosperous rancher.

He had a look at the other man at Morrison's table, a small, thin-shouldered fellow with a hawk nose and small beady eyes. He was dressed in black with a white shirt and a black tie, and from the looks of him he could be a lawyer. His forehead was high, and his thin hair brushed straight back.

A girl came over and Emmett gave his order. He sat back in the chair, looking around the room, and when he caught Halloran's eye, he nodded. The Crown range boss inclined his head slightly by way of greeting, no warmth in the faint smile on his face.

When the waitress came back with his ham and eggs, and a cup of steaming coffee, Emmett knew that by the time he finished his meal he had to make up his mind about Vermilion Valley and Madge Wilson. His better sense told him that he should forget the whole business, take a room at the hotel tonight, and then ride the eastbound to Omaha tomorrow, following his riders.

He needed Madge Wilson's fifty dollars a month about as much as the owner of a large saloon needed a small glass of whiskey. The job meant nothing, and it had been four years since he'd worked for another man. For three successive summers he'd been driving his herds up from Texas, twice to Kansas railheads, and this third summer all the way to Wyoming, where the big profits lay, where local ranchers were stocking up the huge open rangelands, buying cattle at whatever prices they could.

He had no desire to go back to ranching for another man, or for a woman, but the situation here intrigued him, and he was idle anyway the remainder of the winter. Clyde Morrison had a peculiar problem which he had to work out; there was this unusual triangle of Morrison, Dean Brockton, and Madge Wilson.

He was curious about Vermilion Valley, the high winter range which Madge owned, and he told himself he would have a look at it, and make up his mind later what he would do. He tried to convince himself that he was interested in seeing the big snows come to this north rangeland. In his heart he had to admit, also, that he was quite interested in Madge Wilson, even though there were two men in line ahead of him.

CHAPTER 3

It was past three that afternoon when Emmett rode out of Elkhorn. The tough little blue roan, the top horse of the string he'd ridden up from Texas, was well rested and glad to be on the road again.

Moving up the stage road, long since abandoned since the railroad spur connected Elkhorn with civilization, Emmett watched the distant peaks to the north and west. He could feel the cold as the sun lost some of its heat, and he was glad for the new jacket he'd purchased. He'd learned back in town that it was not unusual in this high country to have snow flurries as early as this in the season.

He changed his plans slightly before reaching Morrison's big ranch. Instead of riding past it, and then turning into the road which headed west to Vermilion Valley, he swung west across Crown range with the intention of looking over the land, and then swinging north up to the Pine Tree road, meeting it probably in the vicinity of Vermilion Valley.

As he left the stage road he saw white wisps of smoke rising from Crown, but he couldn't see the buildings. He rode along leisurely, spotting clumps of Crown cattle grazing on the slopes. It was the finest rangeland he'd ever seen, the grass hock-high on his horse, and he could understand now why these northern ranchers were clamoring for more and still more cattle. If a rancher could bring his stock through the winters he'd stand to make a small fortune within a few years.

There was water on Crown range, too, several small creeks which Emmett presumed were branches of Squaw Run. They headed north in that direction.

He made a wide circle, not wishing to come in sight of Morrison's place and having another encounter with the Englishman and his range boss. As he moved west the land lifted in a series of high benches toward the mountains. He passed through several stands of fine timber, all pine and Douglas fir, and when he came out of the timber the second time he dipped down into a small coulee just as the first flurry of snow came.

It was then that he saw the cattle bunched together at the other end of the coulee, probably two or three hundred in number, not scattered for grazing as were the other Crown stock, but deliberately bunched, undoubtedly held together by riders.

Pulling up the roan, Emmett looked down curiously into the coulee. The thin veil of snowflakes drifting across the coulee did not completely conceal the bunched herd, nor the lone rider staring at him from the far end of the coulee.

Some of the stock drifted in Emmett's direction, coming up to within half a dozen yards of him, and he read the brand automatically, assuming it was Crown stock on Crown range. He was surprised to discover that the brand was not a king's crown, the iron of Wyoming Land and Cattle Company, but a hatchet brand.

Emmett stared across the little coulee at the lone rider, quite distinct against the falling snowflakes, and then he saw the gun wink orange in the fading light. The bullet nicked his new leather jacket, indicating that the rider had not shot over his head to warn him away.

The roan jumped with the shot, and the stock at the other end of the coulee fled in Emmett's direction. Angrily, Emmett slipped his own Colt gun out of the holster, but the lone rider had disappeared behind the rim of the coulee. Then he heard horsemen coming down on either side of the coulee, heading toward him, and he realized that he had to ride out of this.

The timber through which he'd just ridden was less than a hundred yards to the rear, and he headed the roan back into it, the little animal scrambling up the grade like a mountain goat.

Two more bullets came after Emmett just as he reached the trees, and stopping, he lifted the Colt and fired twice at the nearest rider, who was just swinging around the rim of the coulee, heading up the grade to the timber.

His bullets didn't hit, but he counted three riders altogether, spreading out as they rode, making for the timber with the evident intention of bottling him up there.

Emmett gave the roan free rein, letting the wiry animal pick its own way through the trees, keeping his head down to avoid overhanging branches. He held the gun in his hand as he rode, but he could no longer see his pursuers.

They were still coming on, though, and he could hear the thud of their horses' hoofs as they plunged through the timber. Emerging on the other side of the woods, Emmett hesitated for an instant and then swung north again, riding parallel to the stand of timber.

His pursuers were undoubtedly expecting him to continue east toward the stage road and off the Crown range. Swinging north again, up in the direction of the Vermilion Valley trace, he thought he could throw them off. With the snow obliterating his tracks, they would have a difficult time following him.

He was riding along the edge of the wood when he heard the other rider plunging toward him, coming out of the timber.

Pulling up the roan, Emmett held the gun steady in his grasp. The second rider, on a bay horse, tore out into the clear less than a dozen yards from the spot where Emmett had stopped. He wore a brown leather jacket and a black hat, and he had a rifle in the saddle holster at his side.

In his chase of Emmett through the timber, this

man had cut north with the intention of intercepting Emmett if he should decide to change his course. His plan had worked, but he apparently hadn't anticipated running into his man so abruptly.

Emmett read the surprise on his face as he grabbed for the rifle in the holster. He didn't want to shoot a total stranger, but there was no other way of stopping him except by putting a bullet very close to him, or wounding him.

Aiming slightly wide of the mark, Emmett fired his first shot just as the rider cleared the rifle from the holster and was lifting it to his shoulder for a quick shot.

The bay horse shifted his position as Emmett's finger squeezed the trigger, bringing the rider into full view of Emmett's gun. With a sickened feeling, Emmett watched the rider suddenly cringe and drop his gun.

As the bay horse moved nervously after the shot, the rider's body fell from the saddle, landing on one shoulder. Emmett knew he was dead even before he hit the ground.

Holstering the gun regretfully, he rode on again, turning the roan into the timber out of which he'd just come, and thus losing his other pursuers.

It was a sobering thought that he'd just killed a man—probably the first man killed in this scramble for winter ranges. It had fallen upon him, a stranger, to spill first blood.

There was little doubt in his mind that these

riders holding the bunch of Hatchet stock in the coulee had recognized him as he rode up. In Elkhorn he'd been tabbed as a Pine Tree rider, and he was wearing a new black leather jacket; his horse, also, was recognizable. He'd ridden this afternoon into something which a Pine Tree rider was not supposed to see, and they'd tried to silence him because of it.

He was frowning as he rode through the timber, coming out again near the coulee. Some of the strange Hatchet stock still lingered in the vicinity.

He stared at the stock, wondering who owned them; why they'd been concealed in the coulee; why men had tried to kill him because he'd accidentally run into them.

The death of the rider with the brown mustache, also, definitely put him on Pine Tree's side if he stayed in this part of the country. He had to side with Madge Wilson now, or buck the opposition alone.

Three miles past the coulee, he came to the trace which led into Vermilion Valley. Now he could see the break in the hills to the north and west, the wide entrance to the valley.

He passed Bar B stock and knew he was on Brockton's range and then he came in sight of the valley. The late afternoon sun tried desperately to break through the veil of snow clouds, and while it didn't succeed it lightened the sky considerably.

Vermilion Valley was broad and deep, a mile

or so wide at the entrance, and running back another ten or fifteen miles into the mountains. The ramparts surrounding the valley were eight and nine thousand feet high, one wall a reddish color, giving the name to the valley.

Running north and south, the high ridge of mountains to the north provided some protection from the heavy snowstorms coming down from Canada, and Emmett could see that while Vermilion Valley would have some snow, it would never be as deep here as on the high plateaus and the open country.

Squaw Run, a small creek not more than fifty yards broad, crossed the mouth of the valley, twisting south at both sides of the entrance. Some distance to the east, outside the valley, Emmett spotted the column which undoubtedly came from Brockton's ranch, and then deeper into the valley, and along the high, red west wall, he saw Pine Tree, a collection of buildings half hidden among the trees at the base of the cliff.

He rode across Squaw Run, the water coming up to the knees of the roan, and as he came out of the water, a man with a rifle stepped from among the willows and watched him thoughtfully.

Emmett rode the horse directly up to him and stopped, looking down at the short, stocky fellow, who wore an engaging grin. He had a flattened nose, his carroty hair curled at the neck. His eyes were blue, like the eyes of a doll. He had on a heavy wool coat and his hat was pulled low over his eyes. He looked down at Emmett, and then at the horse, and then beyond both of them.

Emmett said to him, "Reckon you're loaded for bear."

"Not bear," the short man chuckled. "Four-legged critters with horns on their heads, and two-legged critters following 'em." He looked at Emmett cautiously, and then he said, "Miss Wilson send you out?"

"Asked me to ride out," Emmett nodded. "How many of you are there?"

"Reckon there ain't any more," the short man told him. "Just me—Curly Evans." When Emmett looked at him incredulously, he went on, "Three of us here at night. Other two boys are catching up on their sleep back at the bunkhouse."

"That the whole crew?" Emmett asked him.

Curly Evans nodded. "Had three others, but they drifted. Maybe somebody got to advising 'em." He looked at Emmett curiously, and he said, "They advise you, too?"

Emmett smiled and inclined his head. "Crown rider by the name of Ransom," he said.

Little Evans spat. "The tough one," he scowled. "He push you?"

Emmett rubbed his jaw thoughtfully. "Reckon he didn't push me," he murmured, and Curly Evans grinned.

Pointing to Emmett's saddle, the Pine Tree rider

observed, "That's a Texas rig. They don't push you boys too much, do they?"

"Not while we're breathing," Emmett told him. He took his tobacco sack and paper out of his jacket pocket and started to roll a cigarette, Curly Evans watching him, and then he said, "Who runs Hatchet brand around this way?"

"Old man Wharton," Evans told him, "an' his worthless son, Trev. Two of a kind, both no good. Have a little spread east of the valley."

"Trev Wharton have a brown mustache?" Emmett asked. "Tall, thin fellow, hooked nose?"

"That ain't him by half a mile," Curly Evans stated. "Trev is a big fellow, all shoulders, tow-headed, pig's eyes, no mustache. Why?"

"Man I shot had a brown mustache," Emmett explained. "Three of them rushed me after I ran into this bunch of Hatchet stock held in a coulee on Crown range."

Curly Evans blinked, his mild blue eyes getting wider. "Man you shot?" he repeated. "Dead?"

"Dead." Emmett nodded. "Backed his horse into my lead."

The Pine Tree rider swallowed. "That's one way of putting it," he murmured. "So there's been a killing now! What about this bunch of Hatchet stock on Crown range? Boyd Halloran would hang both Whartons up by their thumbs if he found 'em trailing their beef on his range."

Emmett shrugged. "You ride three or four miles

south of here," he stated, "and you'll find Hatchet stock."

"That's Crown range," Curly Evans muttered. "I ain't figured this out; we better ride back and see Miss Wilson."

Emmett waited for him to bring his horse out of the willows, and then they rode back toward the ranch house, Emmett studying the valley thoughtfully as they moved deeper into it. He said finally, "Good grazing land, and those mountains cut off the worst of the bad weather."

"Best cattle range in the state," Curly Evans boasted. "Every rancher in these parts knows it, too. Ain't one of 'em wouldn't give his eye teeth to have it."

"No water, though," Emmett murmured.

"Plenty of water back there on Bar B range," Evans told him. "Dean Brockton ain't cutting Miss Wilson off."

Emmett was silent the remainder of the way to the ranch house. The Pine Tree ranch was not big, but very solid, a split log affair, rambling in structure, with a veranda across the entire front.

The bunkhouse was to the rear. Behind the bunkhouse were the corrals, a number of horses in one of them.

Madge Wilson came to the door when Curly Evans knocked. She looked at the rider, and then at Emmett, not recognizing him in the new outfit.

"New man rode in, Miss Wilson," Evans stated. "Said you talked to him in town."

Emmett saw her eyes widen then. She stared at him and he reddened a little under her gaze. He saw Curly Evans grinning at his embarrassment, and he said roughly, "Had to buy some new clothes, ma'am."

"Every time I see you," Madge Wilson chuckled, "there's a transformation." She came out and sat on a bench on the veranda. She was wearing the same buckskin jacket with the fringed shoulders she'd worn in town, blue Levi's, and tan boots. She was hatless now, though, and her hair seemed a lighter shade of brown than he'd thought. "Make up your mind about the job?"

"Off-hand," Curly Evans observed before Emmett could speak, "I'd say this hombre had his mind made up for him, ma'am. Shot up a fellow over on Crown range—sounds like Reb Tolivar was the chap he shot—rides for the Whartons."

Madge Wilson looked at Emmett quickly, the smile gone from her face. "What happened?" she asked slowly.

Emmett told her briefly. When he came to the part where he'd shot the Wharton rider, Curly Evans put in slyly, "Claims Reb backed into his bullet, Miss Wilson. They tell me, though, that these Texans can shoot the eye out of a bull at a hundred paces."

Emmett glanced at the little man with some

annoyance. He said quietly, "It was an accident. He had his rifle on me and I wanted to spoil his aim."

Madge Wilson sat very still on the bench, some of the color gone from her face.

"I had hoped," she murmured, "that it wouldn't come to killing. What was Hatchet stock doing on Crown range, and why would they want to kill you?"

Emmett shrugged. "The way I figured it," he stated, "this Hatchet outfit aims to run their stock into your valley tonight. They had the herd bunched in the coulee, and they didn't like it when I ran into them. They had me tabbed as a Pine Tree rider."

"Did you come out here to sign up with us?" Miss Wilson asked him.

"I came to look around," Emmett admitted. "Lot of talk in town about this valley."

"And now," Curly Evans told him, "it's more than talk. It's a dead man, and they got you marked."

Emmett thought about that, and it was not a particularly strong point. He could still pick up and ride out of here immediately if he wanted to, but it was a matter of pride now that he remain in Elkhorn, and a matter of common sense that he line himself up with an outfit, however small.

He said to Madge Wilson, his face expressionless, "I'll take the job, ma'am."

Madge Wilson looked at him steadily. "The job," she said, "is keeping rival cattlemen out of Vermilion Valley. You understand that?"

"Figured that's what it was." Emmett smiled dryly.

"He's kept one out, already," Curly Evans observed, "for good."

Emmett looked at him, and he said no more on the subject.

CHAPTER 4

It was cold that night as they walked up and down the north bank of Squaw Run. Emmett had his leather jacket buttoned up to the neck, and he wore a woolen scarf Curly Evans had insisted he put on before they left the bunkhouse.

"It ain't winter yet," Evans had told him, "but it's coming to it, and you Texans got thin blood."

In the bunkhouse Emmett had met the other two Pine Tree hands—middle-aged Dave Howlett, whom he liked immediately, and a tall, thin rider by the name of Ben Adamson. Both men were old Pine Tree hands, having worked for Madge Wilson's father.

A chill wind blew across the little stream which already had a thin skin of ice. The bank of the creek was covered with the white powdering of snow from the brief flurry of the afternoon. There was no moon tonight, but plenty of starlight. Emmett Kane had never seen the stars so bright as in this northern country.

As they stamped up and down the bank trying to keep the cold out of their feet, Curly Evans said, "Could be you scared 'em off this afternoon, and they changed their minds about coming across."

Emmett didn't say anything. It was a little past midnight now. Dave Howlett was stationed down

41

along the stream to their left, and Ben Adamson to their right. At a signal they were to converge and try to turn the herd back as it came into the stream. Madge Wilson's orders were to fire over the heads of any riders accompanying the herd. She wanted no more killings, but she wanted rival stock kept out.

Commenting upon that fact as they left the ranch, Curly Evans said dryly, "Reckon it might be hard to have both, Emmett. Them boys opened on you yesterday weren't firing high, were they?"

Emmett shook his head. Staring across the stream now, he said to Evans, "Where does Brockton stand in this deal? Anybody comes into the valley has to cross his range first. Wouldn't he try to stop them?"

"He ain't mentioned that he would," Curly Evans said contemptuously. "Been trying to tell Miss Wilson she's worried about something never will happen. How in hell he knows it won't happen I don't know."

Emmett had his own opinions as to why Dean Brockton preferred remaining neutral. Brockton hadn't appeared the type who would relish flying lead even to help out his neighbor, whom he might some day marry.

"That Brockton," the little Pine Tree rider went on tersely, "ain't much from what I can see."

They heard a rider coming up behind them, and peering into the darkness they saw Madge Wilson riding up to the creek. Emmett heard Curly Evans grunt disapprovingly, and when the girl dismounted near them, Evans said tersely, "This ain't no place for you, Miss Wilson. Might be lead flying around here in a few minutes."

"I couldn't stay at home," she told them. "Have you heard anything?"

"Quiet over there," Evans stated.

Then Emmett, standing closer to the creek, felt the slight tremor of the earth, the vibration caused by several hundred cattle on the move. He said briefly, "They're coming now, Miss Wilson. You'd better get back."

"I prefer to remain," the boss of Pine Tree told him.

Emmett just looked at her, seeing her face dimly in the starlight. He walked back into the willows, led the roan out, and mounted. Then he drew his Colt, and sat facing the creek.

They could hear the stock coming on the run now, and very faintly the crisp yells of the drovers.

"Sounds like they're heading straight for us," Curly Evans growled. "Reckon we better bring Dave and Ben up, Emmett?"

Emmett saw Madge Wilson glance in his direction quickly, and he knew what she was thinking. Of the three men working for Pine Tree before Emmett signed on, none of them had the qualities of the leader. They were good men to follow orders, but they didn't move of their own accord, and they were already looking to the new Pine Tree rider for direction.

Emmett said briefly, "We're not sure yet where they'll try to cross. Wait'll they get closer."

He sat in the saddle, loose, relaxed, and he could hear Madge Wilson's quick breathing a few feet to his left. He made a smoke, then, and lighted the cigarette, the match flashing briefly in the darkness.

Curly Evans protested quickly. "Reckon they saw that, Emmett."

"We supposed to be hiding?" Emmett asked him blandly.

The rumble of hoofs came closer, and there was little doubt in Emmett's mind now that the herd was headed straight for their sector of the creek. Lifting his gun from the holster, he fired twice. Then he clicked out the empty shells, inserting fresh cartridges.

Dave Howlett and Ben Adamson arrived just as the first Hatchet stock stepped gingerly into the icy water. Howlett said tersely, "So they're asking for trouble!"

Emmett turned to Madge Wilson. He said quietly, "Better ride back, ma'am. This bunch might fire back at us when we open up."

It was a suggestion, but meant for an order, and Emmett realized immediately that she resented it. He saw her head go up a little, and then she said quietly, "I believe I'll stay with the outfit, Mr. Kane."

Emmett frowned, and then shrugged. "Keep your head down," he advised, and then he rode into the shallow water, the roan crackling the thin ice, and he fired his gun almost into the faces of the stock crowding down around the water's edge on the other side.

Curly Evans, Howlett and Adamson followed him, guns firing, and the noise had the desired effect. The Hatchet stock, about to cross the creek, spun around, doubling on itself, and there was considerable milling with the riders yelling behind the herd, their guns flashing.

Emmett counted four guns, and this surprised him. According to Evans, the Hatchet outfit consisted of only the two Whartons, and Reb Tolivar, whom he'd killed. They'd undoubtedly been reinforced since the encounter with him this afternoon, and he wondered who had provided the reinforcements.

The Hatchet herd had broken and was moving down along the opposite bank, the riders behind them, still trying to drive them into the water. Curly Evans yelled excitedly, "Follow 'em! Run 'em back into the water."

It was Evans's intention to come out of the water and ride down along the north bank of the creek, heading off the stock as it tried to cross. Emmett had a different plan. He called sharply,

"Cross over. We're going after those riders."

Madge Wilson was in the water a few yards away from him. She'd been firing into the water in front of the stock, and he called to her to ride down along the creek, pushing back any stragglers which got across.

He noticed that she hesitated a moment before complying with his request, but she did ride out of the water, and she was galloping her horse down along the north bank when Emmett and the three Pine Tree riders came out of the water on the other shore.

"Give 'em hell," Dave Howlett growled.

The Hatchet riders were still yelling and firing their guns as they raced behind their herd, trying to push them into the water. When the four Pine Tree riders swooped down on them, firing high, they were taken by surprise.

Emmett rode straight for the nearest man, putting two bullets a few feet above his head. The rider swerved. Emmett saw his gun blink in the darkness, and then the bullet grazed his cheek.

Anger surged through him as he bore down on the rider. This Hatchet outfit was still shooting low with the intention to kill. His Colt was empty, and there was no time to reload.

Driving up hard, the blue roan brushing against the other animal, Emmett slashed downward with the barrel of the gun. He heard the other man's sharp yell of pain, saw him slump in the saddle, and then the horse raced away in the darkness.

The milling stock were all around him now, and he had to extricate himself before the excited animals knocked his horse down and he was in real trouble.

He could hear the three Pine Tree riders shooting steadily as they drove on toward the Hatchet crew, and when he got the roan out of the pack he followed them.

The Hatchet stock was trailing back from the creek when he caught up with Evans and the other Pine Tree riders. Curly yelped excitedly, "Ran like hell, Emmett. They didn't figure we'd come across at 'em."

"Always do what they don't figure," Emmett smiled. "Anybody hurt here?"

"Not a scratch," Ben Adamson told him. "Reckon we turned 'em back, Kane."

"May have been a few stragglers got across," Dave Howlett growled. "We'll round 'em up in the morning and send 'em back."

They recrossed the creek and found Madge Wilson waiting for them anxiously. Curly Evans said to her, satisfaction in his voice, "We stopped 'em, ma'am. Now they know there'll be no stock moving onto this range unless we let 'em."

Emmett said, as they were riding back to the ranch house, "How many riders work for the Whartons?"

"Two Whartons, and Tolivar," Evans told him. "Reckon they never needed more than that, Emmett. Hatchet's a small outfit."

"There were four riders driving that stock tonight," Emmett observed, "and Tolivar is dead. Who were the other two?"

"Damned if I know," Evans murmured. "Could be old man Wharton hired two drifters to work his stock tonight."

"Why," Emmett asked, directing his remark to Madge Wilson, who was riding at his side, "would a small outfit like Hatchet be the first to make the attempt to come in here?"

"Possibly they didn't think we'd try to stop them."

"Or else," Emmett told her casually, "somebody bigger than themselves was standing behind them."

"Crown brand?" Curly Evans scowled.

"That herd was bunched on Crown range," Emmett stated. "What do you make of it, Miss Wilson?"

"I—I've never really had any trouble with Mr. Morrison," Madge told him hesitantly, "although I've sensed the fact for a long time that Halloran, his range boss, would like to take over Vermilion Valley."

"Mr. Morrison offer to lease it?" Emmett asked her.

"He made an offer through Halloran during the

48

summer," Madge Wilson stated. "I turned the offer down."

Emmett considered that fact for a few moments in silence as they rode along, the cold beginning to bite into them now. He said finally, "The valley big enough to winter graze Crown stock?"

"Plenty big enough," Curly Evans told him. "If Crown had Vermilion Valley for a winter range, and its own range for summer, they'd become the biggest outfit in this country east of the Rockies. They're plenty big now, but Halloran's afraid to take on more stock because he's worried about these Wyoming winters. Crown lost plenty last winter."

Emmett wondered exactly how much Clyde Morrison, Crown owner, knew concerning these facts. The way it sounded, Boyd Halloran did most of the managing for Wyoming Land and Cattle Company, with Morrison only a shadow in the background.

He wondered, too, why Madge Wilson hadn't accepted Morrison's offer to lease the range for the winter. She could have made a considerable sum of money, and at the same time entailed no difficulty getting her own small herd through the winter. It was coming to him very definitely now that the owner of Pine Tree had a streak of stubbornness in her. She owned Vermilion Valley, inheriting it from her father, and she intended to keep it against all odds. To Emmett it had come as a surprise to learn that Crown had offered to lease the valley, undoubtedly offering a fair rental. If the rental hadn't been fair she would have remarked on this fact.

This trait in the owner of Pine Tree troubled Emmett as they rode toward the ranch house. When they dismounted at the corral and Curly Evans was leading Miss Wilson's horse away, Madge Wilson stepped over to Emmett.

She said briefly, "Will you step into the house a moment? I want to talk to you."

Emmett nodded. He stripped the saddle from the roan, rubbed the animal down, and then left the saddle in the bunkhouse. He saw Dave Howlett and Ben Adamson standing by the fire, warming their hands. They didn't remark on it when he left the house, and Emmett tabbed them as typical veteran cowhands, taciturn, minding their own business.

Madge Wilson had the coffee pot on the stove when Emmett stepped into the kitchen through the rear door. He'd seen the light in the kitchen, and the front of the house was dark.

A half-breed Indian woman did the cooking and the housekeeping for the girl, but she had undoubtedly gone to her own quarters in another part of the house.

Madge glanced at him over her shoulder as he came through the door. She said carelessly, "Sit down. You could stand a cup of coffee, couldn't you?"

"Be obliged," Emmett murmured. He put his hat on the floor and sat down.

Madge Wilson came over and poured the coffee, standing a few feet from him. She'd worn a heavy woolen coat on the ride out to the creek, and she'd taken that off now, along with her hat. The lamplight brought out the color of her hair, a burnished coppery color tonight.

She wore a sweater over the flannel shirt, and the same blue Levi's she'd had on in town. She said as she sat down, "You come up from Texas with a trailherd?"

"That's right," Emmett nodded. He sipped the hot coffee, conscious of the fact that she was watching him steadily across the table.

"They must have paid off pretty well," Madge Wilson commented, "judging from the outfit you bought."

"We made out," Emmett told her. He wondered idly how he could tell her that he had twelve thousand dollars on his person when he'd taken a fifty-dollar-a-month job.

"Were you the trail boss of that outfit?" the girl asked him.

"I had charge of it, ma'am," Emmett nodded.

"You act as if you were accustomed to giving orders," Madge Wilson smiled. "That's the reason I asked you in here tonight."

Emmett sipped his coffee and waited for her to go on.

"The three riders I have can follow orders, but they can't think for themselves. I need a ramrod for this outfit, Kane. Do you want the job?"

Emmett hesitated for a moment, and he saw that his hesitation nettled her a little.

"I'll increase your pay to sixty a month," she said quietly.

Emmett nodded. He was involved in this affair already, and getting himself in a little deeper meant nothing. As a Pine Tree rider he would just as soon give orders as take them.

"Do you want the job?" Madge Wilson repeated.

"Reckon I'll take it," Emmett said.

"Why did you hesitate?" the girl asked curiously.

"Been wondering," Emmett stated casually, "why you didn't lease the valley to Crown for winter graze."

Madge Wilson looked at him sharply as she refilled his cup. "Vermilion Valley is Pine Tree range," she stated flatly. "We intend to keep it that way. If another rancher was in the valley it wouldn't be Pine Tree."

"They'd be out in the spring," Emmett observed. "Crown summer range is just as good as yours."

"I'm not sure they'd go out in the spring," Miss Wilson said tensely.

"No law in this part of the country?" Emmett asked.

"You see any law last night?" Madge Wilson scowled. "There's some law in Elkhorn. Hamp

Freeman is town sheriff. He walks the middle of the road as far as the ranchers are concerned. If it came to a showdown between Crown and myself, who do you think Freeman would side with?"

After a pause Emmett said casually, "You expect any help from your neighbors in this fight?"

Madge Wilson looked at him, frowning. "Bar B is the only rancher I have as a neighbor."

"Reckon he heard that shooting last night," Emmett murmured.

He saw the flush come to her face, and she said tersely, "The wind was blowing the other way. Brockton may not have heard it."

Emmett nodded, his face expressionless. He finished his second cup of coffee, and then he reached for his hat. When he picked it up, she stood up.

"I'm glad you're taking the job," she said.

"I'm obliged for it," Emmett said blandly. "It's good money."

He looked at her as she stood by the door, that slight flush still on her cheeks, making her even prettier than he'd thought she was. He stood for a moment looking down at her, making no effort to open the door, and for the moment he was a man, not a Pine Tree employee, but a man who'd been long on the trail and who'd seen few women.

The girl standing before him was young and exceedingly pretty, and she'd invited him in for a cup of coffee. Emmett Kane looked at her, and she suddenly looked away, and there was an even higher flush on her cheeks. But he knew she wouldn't repulse him, if—

Then he saw himself for what he was, a man who'd done her a favor tonight, and who in the near future might be the means of preserving her loved Vermilion Valley. She was grateful, and she, too, was young and alone like himself.

He turned suddenly, put on his hat and said gruffly, "Good night, ma'am," as he went out.

CHAPTER 5

He was shaving in front of the mirror on the bunk-house wall when Curly Evans came in the next morning. The rider had been watering the stock at the spring at the base of the cliff wall. When he came in with another pail of shaving water to be heated on the potbelly stove in the center of the room, he said thoughtfully, "Heard you was the new Pine Tree boss, Emmett."

Emmett nodded. Both Ben Adamson and Dave Howlett were in the room, and the tall, lean Adamson was stropping his razor as he sat on the edge of his bunk, waiting for Emmett to finish at the washstand. Neither of them said anything, but Emmett had the opinion that they approved of him. They hadn't coveted the job, themselves, and they had their respect for him after last night's affair.

"Any orders for today?" Evans asked him as he set the pail on the stove.

Emmett turned his head, the razor poised. He said, "Dave, you and Ben round up whatever Hatchet stock you find in the valley. Run them back across the creek."

Dave Howlett nodded from the bunk. He went on stropping the razor, but he was listening. Curly Evans said, "What about us?"

55

"We'll ride over to see Hatchet," Emmett told him. He saw Evans start to grin.

"Why?" the little man asked softly.

Emmett shrugged. "Hatchet stock came across Squaw Run last night," he stated. "I'd like to know why."

Both Howlett and Adamson were smiling faintly, even though neither man spoke. Curly Evans had his say, however, a glint in his eyes. "Reckon the day when they pushed Pine Tree around is over, boys."

They had breakfast in the ranch house, the Indian woman doing the cooking for them, too. Emmett followed the others into the kitchen, and thinking of last night embarrassment came over him.

When Madge Wilson walked into the room he felt his face getting red. He scarcely looked at her and he mumbled his good morning. She sat down opposite him at the table, and when he did look at her fully, she was calm, in complete command of herself. She said to Curly Evans, "You'll have to show Kane around and give him the routine we follow, Curly."

Curly Evans grinned. "Reckon he ain't following no routine, ma'am, at least not today."

"No?" Madge Wilson murmured. She looked at Emmett directly, surprise in her eyes.

Emmett moistened his lips with his tongue. "Figured I'd ride over to Hatchet this morning," he said. "Like to ask about that stock tried to cross the creek last night."

"You know why they came over," Madge said slowly.

"Like to have *them* tell me why," Emmett stated, and he saw the grin spread on Curly Evans's flat face.

Madge Wilson acted as if she wanted to say something, but couldn't think of the proper thing to say, and she was silent. Emmett had taken the matter out of her hands. It was something a range boss had to settle, and not the ranch owner. She'd been on the range long enough to know that.

The remainder of the meal was eaten in comparative silence, no mention again being made of the proposed trip over to Hatchet ranch. When the four Pine Tree riders had finished they stood up, nodded to Madge Wilson and went out.

Emmett was at the corral saddling the roan when the girl came up to him. A chill wind swept down from the north end of the valley, and Emmett had his leather jacket buttoned up around his neck. The high peaks of the Elkhorns looked colder than ever, the snow halfway down the slopes now.

Madge was struggling into the heavy woolen coat she'd worn the previous night. She said as she came up, "I wanted to tell you I'm sorry about last night."

Emmett put one boot in the stirrup and went up into the saddle. He looked down at her and said quietly, "Reckon it won't happen again, ma'am." Then he rode off, Curly Evans catching up with him as he passed the corral, and he had the queer feeling that perhaps he'd said the wrong thing.

They crossed Squaw Run, breaking through the thin sheeting of ice again, and they emerged on the other side, heading east as they came out of the valley. Immediately, Emmett sensed the difference. Moving up to the high plateaus, the wind was brisker and colder. He noticed that here at least two inches of snow covered the ground, where they'd only had one inch in the valley.

"Fixing to be a bad winter," Curly Evans stated. "Coming early and hard."

Emmett was watching the thin column of white woodsmoke lifting into the air, being whirled away by the upper breezes. He said, "That Brockton's place?" Curly nodded.

"He could have heard those shots last night," Emmett observed, "if he'd been listening."

"Man would have to be deaf not to hear 'em," Curly Evans growled. "Fight going on on his range and he wasn't man enough to come out and see what in hell it was all about."

"Miss Wilson didn't think he heard the shots," Emmett told him.

Curly Evans spat disgustedly. "Reckon she's trying to think the best of him all the time," he growled. "His dad was a good man. Some day she'll find out, and I hope it's before she marries him."

They could see the Bar B ranch as they topped another rise. It ran along the south bank of Squaw Run, half hidden among a grove of cottonwoods. The ranch house was smaller than Pine Tree, but there seemed to be more outbuildings.

Half a dozen horses stood in the corral near the house, and another horse, a chestnut, was tied in front of the house.

Curly Evans said, "Reckon that could be Boyd Halloran's animal, Emmett. Didn't know he was friendly with Dean Brockton, though."

"Wouldn't hurt to see Halloran," Emmett observed, "and ask him about the Hatchet stock on his range last night."

Curly Evans looked at him, grinning. "Wouldn't hurt a bit," he chuckled.

A horse in the corral whinnied as they came down along the creek, and then the house door opened and Halloran came out, followed by Dean Brockton. They stood on the porch watching Emmett and Curly Evans ride up.

Neither man dismounted. They rode their mounts up to the porch. Curly Evans rolled a cigarette, and said to Brockton, "Meet the new range boss for Pine Tree—Emmett Kane."

Brockton's brown eyes flicked. He was a handsome man with his well-shaped face, his long lashes and sideburns. He nodded briefly.

Boyd Halloran stood against the porch pillar, his big hands in his back pockets, that broad smile on his wide, smooth-shaven face. His turquoise eyes were slightly narrowed, though, and there was no warmth in his smile. He said, "You were promoted pretty fast, Kane."

Emmett nodded. He sat loosely in the saddle, his gray eyes moving from Brockton to Halloran. Then he said without emotion, "I rode across Crown range yesterday afternoon, Halloran, and ran plumb into a herd of Hatchet stock held in a coulee over on your west range. The riders with the bunch jumped me and I had to shoot one of them—a man named Reb Tolivar. Rides for Hatchet."

There was no expression on Halloran's face. He said, "That's right."

"Figured you might know what that Hatchet stock was doing on Crown range," Emmett added.

"I don't know," Boyd Halloran shrugged.

"It's your range," Emmett told him.

"Hell," Halloran snapped, "it's a damn big range; my riders can't cover every foot of it every day."

Emmett looked at him, a faint, cold smile on his face. "Reckon I'd know if two hundred head of strange stock came on my range," he said, and then he turned to Dean Brockton before Halloran could recover. "That bunch of Hatchet stock tried to cross Squaw Run last night, Brockton. We chased them back. You hear the shots?"

"No," Brockton said shortly.

"You're a damned liar," Emmett told him coolly.

Dean Brockton's face went red and then white with rage. He took a step forward to the edge of the porch, standing with his fists clenched. He didn't say anything, and looking down at him Emmett Kane pitied the man.

Boyd Halloran watched from the other side of the porch, saying nothing, looking steadily at Emmett. When Dean Brockton made no move to come off the porch, Emmett turned the roan away, moved around the corner of the house, and continued on toward Hatchet ranch.

Curly Evans was chuckling softly as they rode along, skirting the corral behind the Bar B ranch, moving into the snow-covered meadow beyond.

"Reckon you told him off, Emmett," the Pine Tree rider said after a while.

Emmett shrugged. "Brockton and Halloran pretty good friends?"

"Didn't know that," Evans told him. "Reckon they know each other. First time I ever saw Halloran over this way, though."

As they rode along they saw clumps of Hatchet stock grazing on the bunchgrass, kicking the snow away, and Curly Evans said, "Still Bar B range here. Reckon the Whartons didn't even bother to round up their stock last night after we run 'em back."

They rode on for another mile after leaving

Brockton's place, and then as they were moving up a ridge, a rider came over the ridge and moved down toward them. The horse was a bay with a white face, and the rider used one of those curious English saddles Emmett had seen on Clyde Morrison's big black gelding.

The rider was not Morrison, however. Emmett stared as horse and rider came closer. The rider wore a peculiar, stiff black hat and a tight-fitting black jacket with tan riding breeches.

Curly Evans said softly, "Reckon that'll be Mr. Morrison's sister Pamela."

Emmett lifted his eyebrows in surprise. It was the first intimation he had that Clyde Morrison had a sister in this country. She was within twenty-five yards of them now, and he had a better look at her. Her hair was black and drawn up in a bunch outside that curious, hard black hat. She appeared very slim. A white woolen scarf was around her neck, tucked into the jacket, and her face was flushed and healthy from the ride.

She was smiling at them as she came up, drawing rein half a dozen yards away. She had dark eyes to go with the hair. The features of her face were small, refined, a well-shaped nose, a mouth which reminded Emmett of her brother.

She said cheerily, "Good morning."

She spoke in that clipped, precise way in which Clyde Morrison had addressed himself to Emmett, and Emmett, accustomed to the slow, slurred speech of the South, found it fascinating.

"Morning, Miss Morrison," Curly Evans nodded. Pamela Morrison was looking at Emmett curiously, recognizing him as a stranger in the country. Curly continued, "New Pine Tree range boss, Miss Morrison. Emmett Kane."

Emmett touched the brim of his hat. He heard Curly Evans saying, "Reckon you better be careful not to get too far from your ranch, Miss Morrison. Snow flurries come up pretty quick in this part of the country. I've seen experienced cowhands get lost half a mile from their bunkhouse."

"I'll be careful." Miss Morrison smiled. "Thank you for the advice, Curly." She nodded to Emmett and she said, "Stop in and meet my brother some time, Mr. Kane. We're neighbors of Pine Tree."

"Met him in town," Emmett murmured. "I'm obliged, ma'am."

Pamela flashed them another cheery smile. She nodded and said, "Pleasant ride, gentlemen."

She rode on past them, then, and they could hear the bay's hoofs crunching the snow as she went down the slope. Curly Evans said thoughtfully, "Reckon it won't be so pleasant where we're going, Emmett."

Emmett nodded absently. He said, "Miss Morrison been around this way very long?"

"Came here about a year ago," Curly told him. "Everybody likes her, and the same can't be said about that close-mouthed brother of hers. Rides around like he's cock o' the walk."

Emmett wasn't thinking particularly about Clyde Morrison as they rode on toward Hatchet ranch. He had met a remarkably pretty and vivacious girl, and he was thinking of her dark eyes as he rode along, comparing them with Madge Wilson's gray-blue ones. It was remarkable that within forty-eight hours he'd met two girls in this northern range country who'd appealed to him so much.

They entered timber, emerged on the other side, and then came down again to Squaw Run, a considerably smaller stream here, and sighted Hatchet half a mile to the east.

The spread was about what Emmett had expected, a ramshackle main building with a cluster of smaller outbuildings and pole corrals around it, all of it badly in need of repair, and spread along Squaw Run.

The place seemed deserted, but smoke lifted into the air from the chimney of the main house.

"That's it," Curly Evans murmured. "Ain't much, but that's it." He added contemptuously, "Whartons are two-bit ranchers. Started by stealing a little stock here and there when the ranchers weren't too careful about keeping an eye on 'em. Trev Wharton, though, is supposed to be a rough one."

Emmett didn't say anything. They rode down

along the creek, and they were dismounting in front of the door of the ranch house before they saw anyone. A yellow dog tore around the corner of the house, yapping at them when they came up.

Emmett just looked at the dog, taking no further notice of it. The animal sniffed at his heels for a moment, and then moved away, growling. The man who came out of the house was about sixty, small, shriveled up, with thin, rust-colored hair which stood up on end. He was hatless and tobacco stains showed on his drooping mustache. His trousers sagged at the belt, and his faded, dirty gray flannel shirt was open, despite the cold morning air.

He spat and he said, looking at Curly Evans, "Pine Tree riders?"

"That's right." Curly smiled. "Meet the new Pine Tree ramrod—Emmett Kane."

Old man Wharton spat again. He didn't say anything and he didn't hold out his hand. He looked at Emmett out of small, pinkish, pig-eyes.

Emmett said to him, "Hatchet stock tried to cross Squaw Run last night. Know anything about it?"

Old man Wharton spat again and then he called harshly over his shoulder, "Trev!"

His son came out, a big, hulking man with a small head, bullet-shaped. He had his father's small, pig-like eyes, and the same sandy-red hair. Like his father, he was unkempt, in a dirty brown vest, mud-stained Levi's, a disreputable black hat.

Old man Wharton said to him, a sly grin on his face, "This fellow's talking about Hatchet stock that went across Squaw Run last night, into the valley. Know anything about it?"

"Strays," Trev Wharton grinned. He hitched at his belt, and then tightened it. His hands were big, freckled, calloused.

Emmett looked at him coldly from head to foot as he stood a few yards away from him. He said softly, "The strays had riders behind them, pushing them into the water."

"Don't know a damn thing about that." Trev Wharton grinned.

"Your stock is scattered all over Bar B range."

"Reckon we got drifting stock," Trev Wharton chuckled. "Find 'em all over, mister."

"We'd better not find them again in Vermilion Valley," Emmett told him quietly.

Trev Wharton's grin disappeared. He took a step forward, his heavy jaw coming out. "What'll happen to 'em?" he snapped.

"Nothing," Emmett said. "It'll happen to you."

Trev Wharton measured him. He was a bigger, heavier man than Emmett, and he'd undoubtedly had his saloon brawls. The marks Emmett could see were still on his face, little scars around the eyes and the mouth, a missing tooth, a nose broken at the bridge. He was a rough man with his fists, and proud of his reputation.

"You talk big with that gun on your hip,"

Wharton said tersely. "Let's see you take it off, Jack."

Emmett unbuckled the gunbelt and handed it to Curly Evans. He saw the surprise come into Trev Wharton's pink eyes, and then the small gleam of triumph.

"You're a tough one, are you, Jack?" the rancher grinned. "Now we'll see about it."

He rushed in, aiming a fast blow at Emmett's face. Emmett stepped in fast and hit him a driving punch full on the nose. He heard the bones in Trev Wharton's nose crackle as his knuckles came in contact with them, and then a torrent of blood poured out as the big man staggered back against the wall of the house. He went down on his knees, stunned.

Emmett said to him, "Get up!"

Trev Wharton got up, blood trickling from his chin, reddening his shirtfront. There was doubt in his eyes now, but still some fight in him. He came away from the wall, circling Emmett for a moment, and then rushed in again, diving low, trying to get his arms around Emmett's knees and throw him to the ground.

Emmett brought up his right knee, the hard bone catching Trev Wharton on the forehead. As Wharton's head lifted, Emmett slashed down with his right fist, opening Wharton's cheekbone, a long two-inch cut from which the blood started to flow.

Trev Wharton went down on hands and knees and stayed there, shaking his head.

"Get up!" Emmett Kane told him.

"That's all," Trev Wharton mumbled.

Emmett retrieved the gunbelt from Curly Evans. He saw the father watching him out of slitted eyes. He hadn't made a move since the start of the fight.

Trev Wharton rose to his feet and lurched toward the door holding a handkerchief to his nose. He went inside without a word.

Emmett said to the old man, "Two men jumped me yesterday afternoon as I was crossing Crown range. They were riding herd on Hatchet stock. If it happens again I'll know where to come, and I won't come to use only fists."

Old man Wharton had nothing to say. Emmett turned and walked away from him. When he was in the saddle he said to the old man, "Some day I'll find out who backed Hatchet's play last night, and there'll be hell to pay over there, too."

As they were riding away, heading back toward Vermilion Valley, Curly Evans said thoughtfully, "You figure somebody was behind the Whartons' bid to grab our ranch?"

"The Whartons wouldn't try it alone," Emmett told him grimly. "That Hatchet stock was held on Crown range, ready to move across Squaw Run. Halloran knew about it. The Whartons may have had Crown riders helping them last night, too, but I can't prove it."

"What'll you do when you prove it?"

"We'll let Halloran do the worrying, then." Emmett smiled mirthlessly.

Curly Evans glanced back at the Hatchet ranch house. "Sure," he said softly. "Sure thing, Emmett."

CHAPTER 6

It was past noon when they returned to Pine Tree. Dave Howlett and Ben Adamson were waiting for them in the bunkhouse, having just gotten in. Adamson said laconically, "You boys meet the Whartons?"

"Trev Wharton got himself a broken nose," Curly Evans grinned. "Ran it plumb into Emmett's fist."

Even the silent Dave Howlett chuckled at this, and Emmett said to him, "You get that Hatchet stock back over the Creek?"

"Dozen head," Howlett stated. "We run 'em back."

Emmett stepped over to the stove and held his hands over the hot lid. He said, "Miss Wilson around, Dave?"

"Went into town," Howlett told him. "Wants one of us to bring the buckboard in this afternoon and pick up half a dozen sacks of grain for the stock."

Emmett thought for a moment, and then said, "Reckon I'll go in." He saw Curly Evans grin at Ben Adamson, and he knew what the little man was thinking. The new Pine Tree range boss was hoping he'd ride back from Elkhorn with Madge Wilson.

Emmett told himself that he had an entirely different reason for going into Elkhorn. He wanted to look around a little, to talk to people, possibly to meet the sheriff of Elkhorn. As ramrod for Pine Tree there was much he had to know—about Morrison, about Halloran, about Dean Brockton. Only in Elkhorn, where all the local ranchers congregated, could he learn these things.

At two o'clock in the afternoon Curly Evans harnessed the matched grays and hitched them to the buckboard. Emmett turned the teams down the trace which led to the stage road. The sun had started to melt the light layer of snow, and the trace was slushy. The grays splashed through the soft snow, making good time, and it was about ten minutes before three when Emmett pulled the buckboard up in front of the grain store at the west end of town.

Stepping down from the buckboard, he saw Lee Ransom, the tough, young Crown rider, and another Crown rider, moving past in the muddy street. Ransom gave him a hard glance, but kept going, dismounting in front of one of the saloons close by the hotel.

Up on the walk, Emmett wondered whether he ought to load the grain sacks immediately, or wait until he'd met up with Madge Wilson. He was undecided when Pamela Morrison stepped out of a dry goods store a few doors from the grain store. She walked in his direction, not seeing him at first, and he had no opportunity of avoiding her even if he'd wished.

She was wearing the same riding costume in which he'd seen her that morning on the way to Hatchet ranch, and in the streets of Elkhorn it looked strange.

Emmett noticed that she was not quite as tall as Madge Wilson. Her carriage was very straight, and she moved along the walk briskly, slowing down when she looked at him, recognition coming into her dark eyes.

Emmett touched his hat, wondering if she'd stop to talk. He was surprised and pleased when she did.

"You're Mr. Kane, aren't you?" Pamela Morrison asked.

"That's right, ma'am," Emmett nodded.

"Your accent is new to me," Miss Morrison smiled. "I've been wondering at it. One hears so many different accents in this part of the country. Where are you from, Mr. Kane?"

"Rode up from Texas," Emmett told her, and he saw the interest come into her eyes.

"I've heard so much about Texas," she said thoughtfully.

"Not much like this north country," Emmett observed. "Lot warmer, and no snow in the southern part of it." He looked past her at the distant peaks of the Elkhorn range, and he added, "Pretty up this way, though."

Then he saw Madge Wilson coming toward them, a package under her arm. She'd evidently crossed the street farther up, and had been watching them for some time. He thought she looked rather grim as she came up, but when Pamela Morrison turned around, there was a slight smile on Madge Wilson's face. She said to Emmett, "I didn't know you'd met Miss Morrison, Kane."

"Met her this morning, out near Hatchet," Emmett explained, and he was positive now that his new boss disapproved of his being on such friendly terms with Pamela Morrison. He didn't know, though, whether it was because she was Clyde Morrison's sister, or because she was another woman.

"I've been wanting you to stop in for a visit," Pamela was saying to Madge. "Don't you think you can have tea with us some afternoon?"

"We'll see if we can arrange it," Madge said briefly. To Emmett, she said, "I have a few more purchases to make. You can load the grain on the wagon whenever you're ready."

Emmett nodded. He thought he saw faint amusement come into Pamela Morrison's eyes before she looked away. There was no resentment, no hostility, and Emmett appreciated that. He wondered if Madge was jealous, which would be a very strange thing considering her relationship to Dean Brockton.

"I'll run along," Pamela Morrison said. "Do try to stop in, Miss Wilson."

Madge Wilson said that she would, and Emmett touched his hat briefly. The English girl walked on, turning into another store farther down the street.

Madge said almost brusquely, "How did you make out at Hatchet?"

"Told them not to run any more stock into Vermilion Valley," Emmett stated.

Madge frowned at him. "I was afraid there might be gunplay," she said. Emmett shook his head. He looked down the street in the direction Pamela Morrison had gone, and Madge said tersely, "Wasn't there any trouble at all?"

Emmett rubbed his jaw. "That Trev Wharton broke his nose," he said. When he looked at the owner of Pine Tree she was grinning.

"I'm sorry for Wharton," she said, "but you put it so quaintly."

"Nothing quaint about a broken nose," Emmett murmured, and Madge's grin broadened.

"I'll be ready to leave about dark," she stated. "I have my sorrel in town, but I can ride back in the buckboard, if you don't mind."

"It's your buckboard," Emmett told her. "I'll load."

She walked off, leaving him with his own thoughts, and after a while he stepped into the feed store and with the help of the owner loaded half a dozen sacks of grain to the buckboard.

He had time on his hands after that, and he

moved down along the main street, looking in through the glass doors of the various saloons until he found the one he wanted. Inside the Long Trail Saloon he saw a fat-faced man with a silver star on his vest standing at the bar, chatting with a customer.

Pushing through the door, he moved toward the bar, and it wasn't until he was halfway to the bar that he noticed Boyd Halloran and the little hawk-nosed man he'd seen in the hotel dining room standing at the other end.

Halloran was watching him, a glass half raised to his mouth. He set the glass down on the bar, then, and said something to his companion.

Emmett walked on to the bar, pulling up within a few feet of Hamp Freeman, the sheriff of Elkhorn. He looked at the man in the bar mirror, a chubby man with round cheeks and pale blue eyes, a man with a weak chin, a smooth line of talk, and the ability to make friends and thus acquire votes at election time. He was a man who could stride the fence, antagonize no one, and yet somehow retain his popularity.

Freeman turned his head as Emmett ordered his drink. He nodded slightly, and Emmett returned the nod. The bar was quite empty at this hour. There were only two other drinkers at the long bar with the exception of Boyd Halloran and the lawyer.

As Freeman was turning around again, Emmett

said to him casually, "You the law in this part of the country?"

Hamp Freeman gave him a wide, easy smile. He had good teeth, and when he smiled he was a good-looking man. He said, "That's right, mister."

Knowing he had Halloran's ear, Emmett said blandly, "What happens up this way, Sheriff, when one outfit jumps another's range?"

Freeman moistened his lips with the tip of his tongue. He turned to face Emmett fully, resting one elbow on the bar, his hand fondling the liquor glass in front of him.

"Where'd this happen?" he asked.

"Hatchet stock crossed Squaw Run and came into Vermilion Valley last night," Emmett stated. "Riders were driving them. We chased them back."

Hamp Freeman downed the remains of his drink. "You a Pine Tree man?" he asked.

Emmett nodded. He looked at the glass the bartender set before him.

"See the crew with the Hatchet stock?" Freeman asked. "You see old man Wharton or his son?"

"No," Emmett said.

"Recognize any of the riders?" Freeman wanted to know.

Again Emmett shook his head.

"Hard to take any action," Hamp Freeman stated, "unless we know who was running the stock."

"That right?" Emmett smiled. He looked straight

at Hamp Freeman as he picked up his glass. He was smiling faintly, but it was open, derisive laughter, and Freeman knew it.

His round cheeks stained red. He said stiffly, "What in hell do you expect me to do?"

"I said it was Hatchet stock," Emmett told him easily. "Who would be driving Hatchet stock?"

"Somebody trying to discredit Hatchet," Freeman scowled, knowing it was a weak argument.

The bartender said across the bar, "Trev Wharton came in here this noon with a busted nose, Sheriff."

Emmett Kane downed his drink and put the glass on the bar. He turned then to face Hamp Freeman, and said quietly, "Last night my boys shot high to scare off those riders, Sheriff. The next time they come we'll be shooting low. You can pass that around town."

"Reckon you have a right to defend your range," Freeman said gruffly. "The law will back you up."

"In Elkhorn?" Emmett asked him, "or in Vermilion Valley?"

Hamp Freeman looked at him, dislike on his face. "You're a quick man with your tongue," he said stiffly.

Boyd Halloran, who'd ambled up leisurely, took a cigar from his mouth, and said casually, "He's quick with his fists, too, Sheriff, from what I've seen of Trev Wharton."

The range boss of Crown stood there, heavy

legs spread, his hands in his back pockets, that cool smile on his wide, smooth face.

Emmett said softly, "Even quicker with a gun, Halloran."

Halloran shrugged, and the smile broadened. "Around here it's not healthy to boast of what you can do with a gun, mister."

"I aim to stay healthy," Emmett stated.

"A lot warmer and a lot healthier down in Texas than it is up here, Kane."

There was a very definite warning in the statement, and Emmett knew it. He knew, too, that Boyd Halloran wasn't Hamp Freeman; he wasn't bluff and easy talk; he was a man who would go a long way to get what he wanted, and he wouldn't stop at obstacles in his way. But Emmett wasn't too sure yet just what Halloran wanted.

"Reckon I like it up here, Halloran," Emmett told him.

"Every man to his own taste," Halloran smiled. He nodded to Emmett and to the silent Hamp Freeman, and then went out.

Freeman turned back to his conversation with his friend at the bar, and Emmett paid for his drink and went out. Standing outside on the porch, he watched the few passersby in the street. With the sun beginning to drop behind the Elkhorns it grew cold again, the mud in the street coagulating, a thin skin of ice forming over the mud puddles.

A man came out of a store to throw a blanket over a horse standing at the tie-rack. A dog pattered by, lifting his paws gingerly. Emmett rolled a cigarette and watched the hawk-nosed man with whom Halloran had been speaking cross the street and enter a small store. In gilt letters on the window were the words, "Mark Randall—Attorney at Law. Real Estate & Insurance."

In the short while that he'd been around Elkhorn, Emmett remembered that he'd seen the lawyer twice in the company of Boyd Halloran. It could be that they were merely acquaintances, and it could mean something else. Randall was a lawyer, and he was in the real estate business. Halloran that morning had been paying a visit to Dean Brockton at Bar B, and Halloran had not been known to be friendly to Brockton before.

Watching the dog cross the road, Emmett tried to fit the pieces of the puzzle together, but they fit poorly. He needed more information, and there was the possibility that the little lawyer with the hawk nose could reveal much whether he wanted to or not.

Crossing the road, Emmett moved down toward the lawyer's office and paused at the door, and then went inside.

Mark Randall glanced at him curiously. He was a younger man than Emmett had at first supposed, possibly in his early thirties, but he looked older because of a receding hair line. He had amber-colored eyes and a wedge-shaped face. He said, "What can I do for you, sir?"

Emmett sat down in the chair indicated. The office was small, a cubbyhole of a room which looked out on the street. It was heated with a small potbelly stove, the lid of which was cherry-red.

"You sell real estate?" Emmett asked him thoughtfully. He leaned back in the chair and spread his legs.

Mark Randall lifted his eyebrows. "Looking for a ranch?" he asked curiously.

"I could be," Emmett stated. "Every rider gets tired of working for somebody else."

The lawyer nodded. "You're the man just signed up with Pine Tree, aren't you?" he asked.

Emmett nodded.

"Not staying too long," Randall observed. "Isn't Madge Wilson treating you right?" There was a sly, furtive grin on his bony face as he said this, and Emmett looked at him steadily until the grin disappeared.

"You have anything to sell?" Emmett asked him quietly.

Mark Randall thought for a moment, poking at his chin with a pencil. "Place up on the Wind River," he stated. "Maybe twenty miles from here. Nice place—ranch house, corrals, plenty—"

"Anything nearer home?" Emmett broke in.

The lawyer looked at him. "Where's your home?" he asked softly.

"Vermilion Valley, right now," Emmett said, and saw the grin come over Randall's face again.

"Don't tell me you're thinking of making an offer for Madge Wilson's place. There are fifty ranchers around this way have tried to buy it, the land and the range with it."

"How about Bar B?" Emmett asked.

The question caught Mark Randall by surprise. He'd started to lean back in his chair again, but he came forward quite abruptly, suspicion starting up in his eyes. He said, when he'd recovered himself, "What makes you think Dean Brockton would sell?"

Emmett shrugged. "Don't figure he's making out," he observed, "from the size of his spread. I might do better. He ever put Bar B on the market?"

"No," Randall said shortly. "He's never indicated that he wanted to leave this part of the country. It's understood around here that he'll marry Madge Wilson and they'll combine Pine Tree and Bar B."

Emmett sat loosely in the chair, no expression on his face. "Nice piece of rangeland," he murmured, "and plenty of water. But if he won't sell, he won't sell."

He noticed that Randall was watching him closely, trying to read his mind, and he said, "Anything else around Elkhorn?"

"Not that I know of," the lawyer told him. "If it's just land you want, that's another matter."

"Figured on a ranch," Emmett said, "and range rights. Reckon there's not too much open range left."

"You might find more in Texas," Mark Randall murmured, and Emmett glanced up at him, a faint smile on his face. It was the warning again, the second one this afternoon.

"I'll think about it," Emmett nodded. He got up and went out.

Walking back toward the feed store, he knew he'd hit paydirt in Randall's office. Boyd Halloran, with or without Clyde Morrison's knowledge, was dickering to buy Bar B from Dean Brockton. Halloran may have been using some pressure on the weak Brockton, or very possibly just a high price was sufficient for Brockton to sell out his own place, and in doing so sell Vermilion Valley and Madge Wilson down the river. Pine Tree couldn't exist without the water on Brockton's range.

Remembering the way Morrison had looked at Madge Wilson that first afternoon in Elkhorn, Emmett didn't like to think that he'd be in with Halloran on this deal. It was a cheap, furtive move, and he didn't think Morrison was up to that kind of deal. The Englishman had made his attempt to lease the valley, and now Halloran was making his own deal.

He remembered Halloran's warning, and realized that the man would go far to see that no one interfered with his plans. He was thinking in terms of empire, and the life or death of an unknown Texan who'd drifted into the country meant nothing to him. Very cleverly, he was working both ends against the middle, pushing the shiftless Whartons into a premature attempt to grab the range, and thus making Madge Wilson even more determined to maintain her hold on the valley, harassing her at every opportunity so that she wouldn't lease or sell at any terms.

Halloran's hope lay in a long, tough winter which would wreck Crown brand, and in the secret purchase of Bar B from Dean Brockton, which would wreck Pine Tree.

Emmett Kane realized he could do nothing about the severity of the winter. But there was the possibility he could do something about Dean Brockton.

CHAPTER 7

At dusk Emmett sat up on the seat of the buckboard, smoking a cigar, waiting for Madge Wilson to come up. He'd seen her entering and leaving a number of stores, and once she'd come up to the buckboard to drop a few packages into it.

She came by again as Emmett was relaxing on the seat, and said, "Might be a good idea for you to start on ahead, Kane. I'll catch up with you in a few minutes."

Emmett nodded. As she walked on again he stepped down, untied the grays, and then swung them around and headed north out of town. The wagon wheels crunched on frozen mud in the road. A chill wind was blowing straight at him as he turned the grays into the stage road, and again there was that indefinable smell of snow in the air. He wondered dismally if it snowed every day in this north country.

He was a mile or so out of town, the grays moving along at a slow trot, when he heard Madge Wilson coming up on the sorrel. The night was dark, no moon and no stars, and he couldn't see her until she'd drawn almost even with the wagon. He stopped and waited while she tied the sorrel to the tail gate and then climbed up on the seat.

"Get your shopping done?" he asked.

"Most of it," Madge said. "We like to stock up on

things before the real snow comes along. It might be hard getting in to Elkhorn in another month."

"How deep does the snow get?" he asked.

"I've seen it three feet level." The girl smiled. "When it drifts we really get it."

Emmett sighed. "Must be warm down in Texas," he murmured.

"You'll get used to Wyoming. There's nothing like springtime out this way after a tough winter. It's worth it."

Emmett told her, "You go through an awful lot to get from one season to the next. In San Antonio one season follows the other, and you don't even notice it."

"I'd like to see it some day," Madge laughed.

"Still sticking to Vermilion Valley," Emmett murmured. He glanced up into the dark night sky and said thoughtfully, "What would happen if Brockton ever sold Bar B?"

He knew the question had startled her, because she didn't reply for a moment. Then she laughed. "What put that in your head?" she asked curiously.

"Just wondering," Emmett mused. "Things change. Reckon you'd have to give your valley back to the antelopes if Brockton sold out and your new neighbor closed Squaw Run to you."

"He's not selling," Madge said promptly. "Bar B is his home."

Emmett didn't say anything to that. He'd called Dean Brockton a liar, and the man had only flushed. If someone came along with a check for Bar B in one hand and a gun in the other, Brockton would probably forget all about his home, and all about Madge Wilson.

They rode along in silence for several moments, and then Emmett sat up straighter on the seat and he held his head in an attitude of listening.

"What's the matter?" Madge Wilson asked him curiously.

"Rider coming up," Emmett told her. He'd detected the soft thud of a horse's hoofs some distance to the rear of them.

"Might be a Crown rider," Madge said. "They take the stage road out of Elkhorn."

Emmett nodded. He let the grays move along at a fairly fast pace, and he kept listening, waiting for the rider to come up. He judged the man to be fifty or seventy-five yards behind them.

They drove on for nearly half a mile, and the strange rider came no closer to the buckboard, even though he could hear it rattling along very plainly this still, windless night.

Listening to the measured beat of the horse behind them, Emmett frowned. It seemed almost as if the rider were waiting behind for a purpose. Deliberately, Emmett slowed down the grays along one stretch of the road, and then he listened again, noticing that the rider behind him slowed down too.

"You hear it?" he asked Madge Wilson.

She nodded. She'd been listening, and knew why he'd slowed down. She said quietly, "What do you make of it?"

"Somebody following this buckboard," Emmett murmured. He handed her the reins, and said softly, "I'll untie your horse and slip off the rear of the wagon. Keep the buckboard moving down the road. I'll pull over to the side and let him go by. Then I'll come up behind him."

They never had time to put the plan into execution. Very distinctly, both of them heard the mysterious rider suddenly break into a sharp gallop. The pounding hoofs came closer and closer, and Emmett hauled in on the reins, turning his head to look.

They were on level ground, a straight stretch of road. He could see the wagon tracks gleaming icily in the light of a pale moon, just rising, moving straight ahead of them, disappearing into the shadows. The horseman who'd been following them charged down on the wagon at a full gallop.

Acting instinctively, with the first full sense of impending danger sweeping over him, Emmett grasped Madge Wilson's shoulder. As the horseman tore out of the darkness, Emmett threw himself backward, dragging the girl with him. They tumbled back over the sacks of grain just as a gun roared in the night, the orange flame darting out at them.

Emmett had one glimpse of a rider hurtling by

within a few yards of the wagon. He heard the bullets whisper over his head, and then the rider was gone.

The grays pulling the buckboard broke into a startled run, frightened by the shots, and Emmett had to clamber back to the seat, locate the reins, and gradually bring them to a panting stop.

He looked around at Madge Wilson, sitting among the grain sacks. She said to him briefly, "You see him?"

"Went by pretty fast," Emmett told her. He quieted the horses, and then he stepped to the ground.

"He tried to kill you," Madge Wilson said slowly. "He probably saw you ride out of Elkhorn alone, and he followed you. He didn't know that I'd caught up with you." She was looking at him curiously as he stood beside the buckboard, and then she said, "Who would want to kill you, Kane?"

"I'll find out," Emmett said softly. "I'll have to take your sorrel, ma'am."

"You think it was Trev Wharton, for the beating you gave him this noon?"

"I'll find out," Emmett repeated. "Tonight, or tomorrow, or next year." He walked to the rear of the buckboard and untied the sorrel, stepping into the saddle. He said, "I don't know when I'll be back, ma'am."

He knew quite definitely that he wasn't coming

back until he'd caught up with the man who'd fired those shots at his back after trailing him deliberately for nearly two miles out of Elkhorn.

"You want me to send the boys back here?" Madge asked him after a pause.

Emmett shook his head. "One man rode past here," he said. "One man will go after him." He rode on past the buckboard.

There was no difficulty following the fresh trail in the snow. It ran beside the wagon tracks for a hundred yards, and then swung off to the west, leaving the stage road.

Emmett turned off the road, climbing up a small grade. This was Crown range. He hadn't seen Morrison's spread, but he was sure it lay some distance to the north and west.

The trail from the stage road led due west, crossing open range country, heading up into timber, and then down again to cross a small half-frozen stream.

The rider ahead was moving at a fast pace, taking no pains to conceal his tracks. Emmett skirted a clump of cattle which moved out of his way when he came down into a draw, following the single horseman's tracks.

The smell of snow was still in the air, but it did not snow, and Emmett was grateful. Snow would obliterate those tracks, making it impossible for him to continue the pursuit. He wondered if the man ahead of him had that in mind, or if, perhaps, he was unaware that he was being followed, not having noticed the saddle horse tied to the buckboard as he rode up at that breakneck pace to fire his bullets at the shadowy figure on the seat.

About three miles from the stage road, the trail lifted again to high country, following an old corduroy road through the timber where it was quite dark, the moon's feeble light obliterated. Several times Emmett had to dismount and strike matches to make sure he was still following the trail.

He figured the time to be about nine o'clock in the evening when he came up on a ridge and saw the spot of yellow light below him in a small coulee. He didn't know this country, but he thought they were still on Crown range. The light below could very possibly come from a Crown line camp. The killer had entered the coulee, and the light below gleamed through a cabin window.

Drawing back from the ridge, Emmett dismounted. He rolled a cigarette, touched a match to it, and squatted down on his heels to smoke. The little sorrel was grateful for the rest, because Emmett had been pushing her since they'd taken up the trail. He watched her nosing the snow a few yards away, and then as he smoked he slipped the Colt from the holster, examined it carefully, and replaced it, satisfied.

He had only a conjecture as to whom he would find down there in the Crown line camp. He didn't think it was Trev Wharton. Wharton had fought him standing up, and if he came with a gun, the chances were that he'd come from the front.

Throwing away the half-smoked cigarette, Emmett stepped into the saddle again. He rode along the ridge for a quarter of a mile before descending, coming toward the camp from a different direction.

He could see the faint yellow light from the lamp inside the cabin as he dismounted about two hundred yards away, and then moved forward on foot.

He skirted a small pole corral before he came into full view of the little cabin. A patch of light from the lone window fell across the snow. Emmett walked carefully around the corral, and then he felt the first flake of wet snow strike his cheek.

There was a grim smile on his face as he walked straight toward the cabin door. It was ironic that the snow should have held up just long enough for him to have located the hide-out of the killer. Possibly in another fifteen minutes, with the trail covered by falling snow, he would have had to give up the search.

Off to his right, he could see a lean-to shed and the lone horse standing under it. He didn't bother to look in the window, knowing the man was alone.

Stepping up to the door, he kicked it open suddenly and stepped in, his right hand close to the gun on his hip. He saw Lee Ransom squatting by the fireplace, trying to coax up a blaze. He had his hat off, and his ash-blond hair was ruffled.

Hearing the door burst open, he spun around like a cat, lips drawn back across his teeth, fear in his pale blue eyes. He wore a pearl-handled gun on his hip.

Emmett Kane stood looking at him across nine feet of hard-packed earth floor. There were two bunks in the little cabin, a board table, two chairs. A kerosene lamp stood on the table.

Lee Ransom, the Crown rider, straightened up from his squatting position. Fear made his mouth loose. He just stared at Emmett, knowing why he'd come, and then Emmett said to him softly, "You missed, Ransom."

Lee Ransom's gun was out of the holster, muzzle lifting, when Emmett's first slug tore into him, batting him back against the chimney. He held out one hand to steady himself, a shocked expression on his face, and then he tried to lift the gun again, but Emmett's second bullet caught him in the stomach, just above the gunbelt. He doubled up, the gun dropping from his hand, and he took one step forward, away from the fireplace, before falling like a sack of grain dropped from a wagon.

Behind him, the fire he'd been lighting started to crackle, flame reaching up through the kindling wood. Emmett stood looking down at the dead man, listening to the crackle of the flames.

CHAPTER 8

It was nearly midnight when Emmett crossed Squaw Run, the roan horse breaking through the thin sheeting of ice. The snow had stopped on the ride back to Vermilion Valley from the line camp where he'd left the dead Lee Ransom.

The moon swung up above a ridge of gray cloud in the sky, illuminating the snow-covered valley, revealing the high ridges, black and ominous.

Curly Evans came out of the willows, his hat powdered with snow. He said cautiously, "That you, Emmett?"

"All right," Emmett told him. He didn't dismount as he came out on the north side of the creek. He sat astride the blue roan, looking toward the Pine Tree ranch house, lost in the deep shadows along the high walls. Then he rolled a cigarette and lighted it, Curly Evans watching him thoughtfully.

"Miss Wilson said you was chasing some bucko who'd tried to put a bullet through you."

Emmett nodded. He puffed on the cigarette, got it going, and tossed the match away, watching it splutter out in the soft snow. He said, "It was Lee Ransom."

Curly Evans swore softly. "That hombre's headed for trouble, Emmett."

"He got it," Emmett murmured, and he started

on. There was silence behind him as he rode toward Pine Tree ranch.

The parlor lamps were on, and he knew that Madge was waiting up for him. He didn't particularly want to talk to anyone at this time, even Madge, but it wouldn't have been proper to go on to the bunkhouse and turn in after he'd seen her light.

Stabling the roan, he went up on the porch, and the door opened as his boots sounded on the wood. Her hair was done up for bed, and she wore a green wrapper which brought out the rich color of her hair.

"I have hot coffee for you in the kitchen," she said.

Emmett took off his hat, stamped the snow from his boots on the porch floor, and followed her into the kitchen, noticing that she was considerably smaller with her high-heeled boots off.

She was pouring the coffee when she asked the question. Emmett took the chair on the other side of the little table. He dropped his hat on another chair in the room, noticing the small layer of melting snow on its flat crown.

"You find the man?"

Emmett stirred the hot coffee with a spoon, looking down into it. "Trailed him to a Crown line camp," he said. He sipped the coffee and put the cup down. The hot coffee warmed him after the cold night ride. He felt some of the tension begin to leave him, and he realized that since Lee Ransom had fired those shots at him in the buckboard, he'd been wound up tighter than a drum.

"Who was it?" Madge asked.

"Lee Ransom, Crown rider."

Again he stirred the coffee without looking at the girl.

"You're all right—then he's dead," she commented slowly.

"He's dead," Emmett nodded.

Neither of them spoke for some time. He noticed that she hadn't poured coffee for herself, and the thought came to him that she'd already had hers—perhaps more than one cup, while waiting for him to return.

When she spoke she had control of herself again. She said, "Why would Ransom want to kill you?"

Emmett looked at the floor. "Ransom didn't like me," he said. He had his own private theory as to why Ransom had followed him and tried to put a bullet through his back. It could have been more than plain dislike, or even hatred. Ransom was a Crown rider, and he took orders from Boyd Halloran. There was the possibility that Halloran has ascertained from the lawyer Randall that Emmett Kane was interested in Brockton's Bar B. That was reason enough for him to want Emmett Kane out of the way, along with the fact that the new Pine Tree ramrod was getting into his hair.

"You don't try to kill everybody you don't like,"

Madge Wilson was saying, "but I don't believe Mr. Morrison sent Ransom after you."

Emmett shrugged. "You figure Boyd Halloran asks Morrison every time he wants to shave his face?"

"I can see Halloran ordering it," Madge murmured, "but not Morrison. What can we do about it?"

Emmett shook his head. "Been done," he said. "You can't prove anything with Lee Ransom."

"There'll be others," Madge told him. "You know that."

Emmett had thought of that, too. Killing one man didn't destroy a brand. If Halloran had sent Ransom, he would send others—maybe better men, men who made killing their business, and one of them would catch up with him sooner or later. Emmett considered this situation bleakly, wondering why he hadn't ridden back to Texas, and why he didn't leave now while he was still alive. In two days he could be in Omaha and aboard a train taking him out of this mess.

"I don't want to see you killed," Madge Wilson said. "You know that."

Emmett looked at her, remembering that she was supposed to be engaged to Dean Brockton. The way she was looking at him now that engagement was already abrogated. He knew he couldn't leave. This girl with the gray-blue eyes had a hold on him, and yet there was something about her which repelled him. Back in town he'd learned that she was ambitious, a driver. She wouldn't open up the valley for winter graze at any cost, even though she knew that it would stop the bloodshed—maybe the shedding of his own blood.

He wondered if it was possible that she, like Boyd Halloran, was power-mad. She wanted an empire established here in Vermilion Valley, and she wanted to control it. She wanted to see her stock filling the big valley, overflowing to the adjacent ranges. Maybe that was why she was marrying Dean Brockton—a weak man. She had to be the boss.

"I don't aim to get killed," Emmett said. Looking across the table at Madge Wilson he found himself thinking about another girl—a girl with a strange, entrancing way of speaking, a girl with black hair drawn in a bun at the back, a girl with laughing black eyes. He started to wonder if he were staying around for Madge Wilson's sake, or for the sake of this English girl, the sister of the man they were fighting.

"I just want you to be careful," Madge murmured.

Because without me, Emmett thought bleakly, you're licked?

He knew that that was unfair. As yet he knew too little about this girl to arrive at such conclusions. Possibly she was just bewildered, backed up against a wall, and stubborn only because she knew she had to fight or go down.

Tonight, looking across at him over the little table, she was all woman, very soft, very alluring. Then she put out a hand and placed it on top of his, resting on the table beside the coffee cup. She said softly, "I'm glad you're with us, Emmett."

He would have kissed her, but he remembered Dean Brockton, and before he could do anything she took her hand away. He stood up and reached for his hat, a trickle of water running from it when he picked it up.

"I'll turn in," he said. "Obliged for the coffee."

"I had to wait up," Madge said. She was watching him, and he wondered if she were disappointed because he hadn't done anything after she'd touched his hand. Her face revealed nothing. She stood by the table, one hand touching it, the other at her side. She looked very young, very girlish with her hair done in braids, drawn back around the ears, and in that too-large green wrapper.

He walked to the bunkhouse, finding Curly Evans just coming in from his watch on the creek, and Dave Howlett going out.

"No trouble tonight," Curly observed. He looked at Emmett, pulling off his boots as he sat on his bunk across the room, and he added wryly, "Not around here, anyway. . . ."

In the morning the sun was bright and warm, melting the snow rapidly, leaving bare patches of brown all over the valley. It was almost like a spring day, and the change was amazing to Emmett, who was anticipating increasing cold and more snow.

"Fools you some," Curly Evans admitted, "but it ain't winter yet, Emmett. This is still part of our summer. We get a late start in the spring."

There was mud underfoot now as Emmett made a circuit of the valley, looking over Madge Wilson's small herd. He ascertained the fact that there was no entrance into the valley except across Squaw Run. A man on foot could climb some of those steep ramparts, but no animal ever would, and it meant that Vermilion Valley was safe for Madge if they could prevent stock from crossing the creek.

Earlier in the morning Emmett had sent Dave Howlett into town with a message to Hamp Freeman telling of Lee Ransom's death. He wondered what Freeman would do about it, and what Boyd Halloran would do.

He was a little surprised, on returning to the ranch house, to see Halloran and Clyde Morrison riding up. At this early hour of the morning they had probably not been to town, which meant that neither man knew yet of Ransom's death.

Turning the roan out into the corral, Emmett watched Halloran and Morrison dismount in front of the house, and Madge Wilson come out. He noticed that she looked in his direction before greeting the two men, and he wondered if she expected him to come over and take part in the discussion. He decided to wait until she asked him, and stepped into the barn to roll a cigarette.

Curly Evans was pounding on a horseshoe, and he looked up and grinned when Emmett came in.

"Reckon the Englishman's gonna make another try to lease this winter range," he observed. "Won't do him any good. Miss Madge makes up her mind, and it's made up. Ain't nothing changing it."

Emmett didn't say anything to that. He leaned back against a stall post to watch the other work, and then Ben Adamson stuck his head in and said laconically, "Boss wants to see you, Emmett."

Emmett threw away his cigarette as he came out through the opening. He noticed that Halloran and Clyde Morrison hadn't been invited inside, but were standing on the porch, both men with their hats in their hands. Madge Wilson stood to one side of the door. She was hatless, but she wore a checked woolen jacket.

The Englishman turned to look as Emmett crossed the yard and came up the steps. Morrison's heavy bulldog jaws were set grimly, but there was a perplexed expression in his black eyes. Looking at him, Emmett realized he was a man who always wanted to know exactly where he stood on every issue, hating doubt and uncertainty. If he were in love with Madge Wilson, it was perhaps the first time in his life he'd experienced the emotion, and it annoyed him because he was unable to make any headway with a girl who had to be at odds with him.

"Emmett," Madge said, "Mr. Morrison has just

made another offer to lease the valley for the winter."

Emmett looked at Morrison and then at Boyd Halloran. His eyes lingered for a moment on the big, solid, blond man. He didn't know for sure that Halloran had sent Lee Ransom after him, and there was the possibility that he never would know with Ransom dead; but Ransom hadn't appeared to be the kind of man who would take a chance like that without some reasonable profit from it, much as he hated Emmett Kane.

Halloran was smiling faintly as he looked at Emmett. He nodded, but he didn't say anything.

Emmett asked Madge Wilson, "You taking the offer?"

"No," she said flatly, and he wondered why she'd called him out. He found out immediately. "I don't believe," Madge went on grimly, "that these gentlemen are aware of the fact that a Crown rider attempted to murder us last night."

Emmett knew, then. He was the big stick she was using against Crown brand, and she wanted them to know it.

"Murder?" Clyde Morrison choked. He looked at Halloran, and Halloran shook his head slightly. The Crown range boss looked at Emmett, then, and his face again showed nothing, but his turquoise eyes narrowed.

"Who tried to murder you last night?" Halloran asked pleasantly.

"Lee Ransom," Madge told him.

Emmett was watching Clyde Morrison's face. The Englishman's jaws were clamped shut, and his thick, short-fingered hands were tight at his sides.

"You are making vague accusations," Halloran smiled. "Where is young Ransom?"

"Dead," Emmett told him. "You'll find him in one of your line camps."

Halloran's eyes seemed to become a shade lighter, but he was still smiling.

"That Ransom," he said softly, "was a damned fool. He never liked you, did he, Kane?"

"No," Emmett admitted. "It happened that Miss Wilson was in the buckboard with me last night when Ransom opened up on us with his pistol. We were fortunate none of the bullets went home."

Morrison said slowly, "I regret this incident very much, Miss Wilson. Unfortunately, there is nothing I can do about it now to make amends. Will you accept my sincere apologies?"

"You can do something about it," Emmett said casually, and Morrison turned to look at him.

"What is that?" he asked.

"Find the man who sent Ransom after my scalp."

Clyde Morrison looked at him, puzzled, and Halloran said as he flipped the cigar butt into a bank of melting snow just off the porch, "What makes you think somebody sent Ransom?"

"I just figure he was sent," Emmett said evenly.

To Morrison he said, "When you find the polecat, tell him to come himself the next time."

"Could it be, Kane," Halloran purred, "that you are making an issue out of a personal affair, and trying to involve Crown brand and Pine Tree?"

"I don't think so," Emmett told him. "Some day I'll know for sure."

Clyde Morrison said to Madge Wilson, as if anxious to get her back into the conversation, "Are you still rejecting my offer to lease the valley, Miss Wilson?"

"Vermilion Valley is Pine Tree range," Madge said flatly. "I intend to keep it that way."

"I had hoped," Morrison said, "that we could become good neighbors, Miss Wilson."

Emmett saw Madge Wilson glance at him curiously. The Englishman's wide face was ruddier than usual, and he didn't look at her. Emmett understood that this was about as much as Morrison could unbend. He was a stiff man, and a pompous one, and for him falling in love was a predicament.

"We'll be good neighbors," Madge Wilson said, "as long as Crown brand stays on the other side of Squaw Run." She was still looking at Morrison, and Emmett could see that the Englishman's remark had stirred her a little.

Morrison and Halloran went back to their mounts and rode off, Emmett and Madge Wilson watching them from the porch. Madge said thoughtfully, "I don't think Mr. Morrison knows what's going on most of the time at Crown. This is all new to him, but he likes cattle and he likes the country."

"Throw in with Crown," Emmett said, "and you two control the best rangeland in these parts— summer and winter graze." He added idly, "Of course that leaves Brockton's Bar B sandwiched in between."

Madge Wilson frowned at what she considered the levity in his voice, but he knew that she was thinking of that prospect. It was the ideal setup for a northern rancher—plenty of rangeland, water, and winter graze. When other ranchers were frozen out, they prospered; when the price of beef went sky-high after a tough winter, they stood to reap enormous profits.

"You hinting at a partnership between Crown and Pine Tree?" Madge murmured.

"They have other names for it," Emmett told her, and he saw her flush a little; and when she did this she was a young girl who needed help, and he was there to give it. She was not clever and hard and a driver using him as a big club. Maybe she was that, and maybe she was the other thing, and Emmett Kane didn't know for sure which part of her was the real Madge Wilson. He knew this, though—that he had to stay around to find out, even if staying around meant he'd find himself some night with a bullet in his back.

"I'll make my own matches when I'm ready to make them," Madge said almost stiffly.

"Your life," Emmett nodded. "I'm just riding along, ma'am."

He went back to the barn and he watched Curly Evans for a while, and then he squatted in the warm sun on the south side of the barn, smoking another cigarette. When he'd finished, and the iron had sounded announcing dinner, he'd made up his mind. This afternoon he would ride over to see Dean Brockton, owner of Bar B.

CHAPTER 9

Madge Wilson was hanging some clothes on the line behind the house when Emmett rode off that afternoon. She saw him going and raised a hand to him. He knew she was wondering what his purposes were now.

There was very little to do at Pine Tree these early winter days, and he'd been signed on largely to keep rival stock out of the valley. Besides, it was understood that as ramrod for the outfit he came and went as he pleased.

Even Curly Evans's curiosity was piqued as he watched Emmett saddling the roan before riding off. Curly hinted at going along, but Emmett didn't rise to the bait, and Curly went back to his horseshoes regretfully.

The ice was gone from Squaw Run as Emmett pushed the roan through the hock-high water, coming out on the other side, the horse blowing and snorting from the chill water. He ran across a scattering of Bar B stock on the other side of the creek, and then swinging up over a low ridge he saw the white woodsmoke from Brockton's ranch house lifting up into the still air.

An old man with a limp came out of the corral as Emmett rode up, looked him over leisurely, and then said, "The rough man from Pine Tree!"

He grinned toothily as he said it, and there was respect in his faded blue eyes. Emmett said to him, "Brockton around?"

"Went in to Elkhorn," the old man told him. "Might be getting back any minute." He spat and he said, "You want to set?"

"I'll look around," Emmett said. He dismounted, tying the roan to the corral.

The old man watched him, and then he took out a stub of cigar from his shirt pocket and put it in his mouth. He said, "You ain't the only one's been looking around, mister."

"That right?" Emmett murmured. He slipped a fresh cigar from his shirt pocket, inside the leather jacket, and stuck it in the old man's hand. He was walking past him toward the porch when he heard the old man say, "Obliged, tough man."

Emmett sat down on the porch. He said, "How many head does Brockton have?"

"Near five hundred," the man said. He was lighting up the cigar as he came over and sat down on the bottom step of the porch stairs.

Emmett put a cigar in his mouth, but he didn't light it. He said, "Brockton's not much of a rancher, is he?"

The old man looked up at him as he puffed on the cigar. "Ain't much of anything," he growled.

Emmett looked across the rolling hills, the grass gray and seared now, but he could imagine it in midsummer. He said, "Pretty good range, though."

"Not as big as Crown brand," the old man stated, "but he's got something Morrison and Halloran ain't never had."

"Winter range," Emmett murmured.

The old man nodded. "Soon's the big snows come Bar B stock drifts into Vermilion Valley. Agreement between old man Wilson and Brockton's pa."

Emmett touched a match to his cigar, sat back in the chair contentedly, and then said, "How much did Halloran offer for Bar B?"

The old man glanced at him quickly. "How in hell did you know Halloran's trying to buy us out?"

Emmett shrugged. "Figured it out," he said.

"Figure out his price, then." The old man grinned. "I ain't supposed to know anything."

"You the only hand at Bar B?"

"I'm Ben Keefe," the man told him. "Everybody knows me. Me and Dean Brockton work Bar B alone."

Both men sat silent for a while, smoking, and then Ben Keefe pointed with his cigar. "Brockton's coming up now," he said.

Emmett saw the buckboard topping a rise half a mile away, coming down the trace from Elkhorn. Ben Keefe got up, flicked ash from his cigar, and moved down toward the corral.

Dean Brockton drove the buckboard in under a shed behind the house, giving Emmett a searching look as he went past. When he came around to the front of the house, Emmett was still sitting on the porch, the cigar in his mouth.

Brockton came up on the porch and put his back against one of the uprights. There was a grim expression around his weak mouth, and his brown eyes were hard. He said, "I don't take this to be a friendly visit, Kane."

Emmett smiled and shook his head. "This is business," he said.

Dean Brockton looked at him, a little puzzled now. He started to roll a cigarette, and Emmett noted the slender hands, long-fingered, blue veins showing in them.

"Get to it," Brockton told him.

"What's your asking price on Bar B?" Emmett said.

He saw Brockton's brown eyes widen, and a few grains of brown tobacco spilled on the porch floor as he rolled the cigarette and put it into his mouth.

"What?" Brockton said.

"I believe Bar B is for sale. I'd like to make a bid."

"You're crazy," Brockton mumbled. "Who said I'm selling out?"

"I did," Emmett told him. "To Boyd Halloran."

Brockton touched a match to his cigarette and got it going. He didn't speak right away, and Emmett knew he was trying to figure things out, this quick approach having unsettled him. He'd recovered himself now, and he was smiling contemptuously as he spoke.

"You say you want to make a bid for Bar B. You must have made a quick pile since you signed up with Pine Tree a few days ago. I'd like to see the color of your money?"

"You ask to see Halloran's?" Emmett murmured.

"I never said Halloran made a bid for my ranch," Brockton growled. "You're barking up the wrong tree, Kane."

"Let's bark up this tree, then," Emmett smiled. "If you could get more for Bar B from me than from Halloran, why not take it? You're pulling out of this country anyway."

He saw the cigarette droop in Brockton's mouth, and the first evidences of greed come into his brown eyes. He knew he was on the right track.

Brockton said belligerently, "Who the hell says I'm pulling out?"

"If you sold Miss Wilson down the river," Emmett observed, "you couldn't stick around here."

"I never said I was selling anything," Brockton said sulkily.

Emmett shrugged. He sat in the chair, smiling, saying nothing, letting the pressure weigh upon Brockton. He was quite sure he had his man now. Brockton had talked with Halloran about selling his place, and he had planned on leaving Elkhorn. It meant that Madge Wilson meant nothing to him, that he was no rancher to begin with, and that he wanted to get out of this country. Halloran was giving him a way out, but now another man had come along who might up Halloran's price.

"You're wasting your time here, Kane," Brockton muttered.

Emmett got up. He took one step forward, and Brockton said, "Miss Wilson know anything about your coming here?"

"She wouldn't believe it," Emmett said, "if I told her you were figuring on selling Bar B. She doesn't think I have the money anyway to buy my own ranch."

"Have you?" Brockton asked doggedly.

Emmett smiled at him. "What's Halloran's bid?"

Dean Brockton took a deep breath. "Four thousand dollars," he said.

"I'll give you forty-five hundred," Emmett said without batting an eye, and then he reached inside his jacket, took the bank draft from the shirt pocket where he'd buttoned it, and held it up in front of Brockton's eyes. The draft was drawn on the Elkhorn National Bank.

Dean Brockton sat down on a wicker chair on the porch. He took off his hat and held it in his hand. Emmett noticed that his face was pale, and that he was breathing faster than usual. He said slowly, "For five hundred dollars I might have my head shot off. Why should I take that risk? You know Halloran."

Emmett shrugged. "Forty-eight hundred," he offered, "and that's my last bid." He knew Bar B was worth that much. He added, "We can run up to Aspen City and put the deal through without anyone's knowing. I'll give you a week to clean up your business here, and you'll be a thousand miles away when Halloran finds out about it."

Dean Brockton sat there, his hands loose in his lap, the cigarette sagging in his mouth. Emmett said to him, "You don't owe Halloran anything."

Brockton frowned. "No," he said.

"Where can I meet you in Aspen City?" Emmett asked.

Brockton went off on a new tack. There was a little bluster in his voice as he spoke. He said, "You're not figuring on cutting off the water rights to Pine Tree, are you?"

Emmett looked at him. "You ask Halloran that?" he said, and he saw the color come into Brockton's smooth brown face.

"I don't want to see Madge squeezed out," he muttered. "That's all I'm worrying about."

"She won't be squeezed out," Emmett assured him, "but that won't be for you to say."

The curiosity was in Brockton's eyes now. He said thoughtfully, "Kind of wondering why you're doing this, Kane."

"I like Bar B," Emmett told him.

"Could it be," Brockton grinned, "you like Bar B's neighbor, too?"

"We have a deal?" Emmett asked thinly, "or do I ride away?"

"I'll be in the Longhorn bar in Aspen City tomorrow afternoon," Brockton told him. "Have that draft with you."

Emmett nodded. He went down the steps and walked to the corral to untie the roan. Brockton was still watching him as he rode away. Old Ben Keefe was watching, also, from under the wagon shed, the cigar Emmett had given him still in his mouth.

Instead of returning to Pine Tree in Vermilion Valley, Emmett rode due south. Leaving Bar B behind him, he came out into open country again, and the high rolling plateau of Crown range. He saw Crown stock as he climbed a grade sparsely covered with timber, and when he'd gone over the rise and was angling down toward a small stream he saw smoke lifting from a point south and west, and he identified this as the Morrison place.

He found himself thinking of the English girl again, and this was strange, because he'd just spent nearly half of his wealth buying a ranch he didn't particularly want, in order to protect another girl. The investment, however, had been a good one. If he made up his mind to remain in this northern range country he had a good spread to begin with, and if he did not he could always sell Bar B, and maybe at a profit.

At the stream he let the roan drink, dismounting

to stretch his legs a little. He walked up the stream a short distance and came back, and then he saw three riders moving down through the timber out of which he'd just come, heading straight for him.

He was sure they'd spotted him from a distance as he went up the grade, and had followed him, for what reason he couldn't guess; but the horse he rode was easily identifiable at a distance.

As the three riders came toward him he noticed that one of them had a peculiar white patch across the bridge of his nose. He remembered Trev Wharton's broken nose of a few days back, a nose which would be straightened and held in place with adhesive tape by now.

The three riders came on steadily, and as they drew closer Emmett recognized old man Wharton with his hulking son. The third man he did not know; he was a short, rat-faced fellow, who might be taking the place of the Hatchet hand Emmett had shot.

The Hatchet riders stopped a dozen feet from Emmett as he stood on the ground, the roan having just come out of the water. He was anticipating trouble of some kind, but he was not sure yet what form it would take. Trev Wharton had had his beating, and he wouldn't want any more of that. Of the three, only the rat-faced fellow carried a gun, and he didn't look like a man who could be particularly dangerous with a gun; and then Emmett had a glimpse of his hands as the dapple gray horse he was riding shifted position.

The small man's hands were slim and brown, not the hands of a range rider, and looking at those hands Emmett Kane knew from what direction the danger would come.

The little man on the dapple gray was grinning at him, revealing yellowed, pointed teeth, and then the big gun in his holster came out with an easy, effortless swish of the right hand. Emmett found himself looking into the muzzle of a Colt .45.

"Hold it there, Pete," Trev Wharton grinned.

"He ain't moving," Pete chuckled. "He's just standing there, ain't he?"

Emmett didn't say anything. He watched Trev Wharton getting down from his horse, and he knew now what it was all about. Old man Wharton was watching him, leaning forward a little, his pig's eyes blazing, mouth open a little.

Trev Wharton came forward slowly, and Emmett said to him, "You have another nose you want busted, Wharton?"

"Bustin's on the other side now," Trev murmured. "Drop that gunbelt, Kane, and you watch him, Pete Cooley. He's slicker'n hell."

"He moves," Pete grinned, "and he's dead."

Without looking at the rat-faced man on the horse, Emmett said to Trev Wharton, "You tell your boy the next time he draws a gun on me he'd better use it right off."

"Why?" Pete asked.

"You'll be dead, otherwise," Emmett said.

Trev Wharton stopped five feet away from Emmett. "Told you to drop that gunbelt," he said.

Emmett made no move. Trev's scuffed brown leather jacket was open, and inside the jacket Emmett caught a glimpse of a short length of iron pipe. He realized, then, that this had been no chance meeting. Trev Wharton had come looking for him, and he'd come prepared.

"You're a tough one, Wharton," Emmett murmured, "when you come with a crowd."

"You hear what I said about that gunbelt?"

Emmett glanced at Pete Cooley, whose small eyes were narrowed, greenish in color, watching him intently. The Colt was steady in his hand, and he was a man who loved to use it.

"Get to it, Trev," old man Wharton growled.

Trev Wharton took another step forward, which he should not have done. The extra step brought him within reach of Emmett, and Emmett realized that he had to make his move now, or absorb the worst beating he'd ever get in his life.

He looked down at the gunbelt as his fingers worked on the buckle, and then before he could unhook it, he leaped forward straight at Trev Wharton, diving low and catching him around the waist.

Wharton yelled and slashed down with his right hand at Emmett's head. Emmett got his left shoulder into the man's stomach and kept digging with his boots, driving Wharton back, and then rolling with him when he went down. He knew that Pete Cooley wouldn't risk a shot with them rolling on the ground, even at close range.

Old man Wharton shrilled, "Get him, Trev."

Trev was cursing, beating at the top of Emmett's head with both hands as they twisted and squirmed on the ground. Emmett kept his head in against Trev Wharton's chest, waiting his opportunity, at the same time slipping the gun from his own holster. He had a glimpse of Pete Cooley on the dapple gray, backing the horse away, the gun moving in his hand.

As he rolled he got the gun clear, and he fired in the general direction of the little gunman, hoping to drive him farther back. The shot had the desired effect. Cooley moved the gray away from Emmett's gun, knowing that Emmett had the big advantage now with a gun in his hand, and protected to some extent by Trev Wharton's body.

Trev seemed to recognize his danger, and he screamed, "Don't shoot, Pete!"

At that moment Emmett suddenly lunged up with his head, catching Trev Wharton squarely on his injured nose. The man screamed with pain and went limp. He rolled away, blood trickling from his nostrils again, and Emmett came up on his knees, gun pointed in Pete Cooley's direction.

Cooley wisely had retreated another fifteen yards, and the gray was standing on a little knoll.

He had his gun on Emmett, and Emmett had his gun on him. They stared at each other for a long moment, and Emmett realized that Pete Cooley didn't like this situation at all, since he was the better target.

Trev Wharton was moaning to Emmett's left, still sitting on the ground, all the strength gone out of him. Old man Wharton's horse had backed away after Emmett's shot, and Emmett could hear him cursing senselessly, but taking no part in the fight.

The seconds ticked away as the two men stared at each other across the intervening space, and then a rifle cracked from the stand of timber on the other side of the stream. The bullet kicked up dust in front of the gray horse, and Cooley was nearly unseated as the animal reared up, snorting.

There was another shot, and then Cooley tore away toward the west, crouched low in the saddle. No more shots came from the timber.

Emmett kept his gun in hand, watching Trev Wharton rise to his feet, holding a bloody handkerchief to his nose, and wobble toward his horse. The two Whartons followed after Cooley, though with less haste, and when they'd topped a rise, disappearing from sight, Emmett turned, expecting to see one of the Pine Tree hands coming out of the timber.

The horse was a bay with a white face—Pamela Morrison's horse. She'd put the rifle back into the saddle holster, and she rode toward him cheerily, the strange little black derby hat perched on the side of her head, wearing the tight-fitting jacket and the white silk scarf.

"I heard shots," she said, "and I came to investigate."

Emmett smiled faintly. "Pretty good shot, yourself," he observed.

"My brother taught me to use a gun. But I'm not very good at it."

"I'm obliged to you," Emmett said. "You figure I was in trouble?"

"You were on the ground, and there were three of them. It wasn't sporting." She sat there, looking down at him, the curiosity in her eyes. "Who were they?"

"Hatchet brand," Emmett said briefly. "Neighbors of yours."

"Not very pleasant neighbors," Pamela grinned. "I'm glad we have not been formally introduced."

Emmett stepped up into the saddle and turned the roan back across the stream, Pamela Morrison riding with him.

"They're not very pleasant," Emmett agreed.

"Would they have killed you?" Pamela asked him.

Emmett shrugged. "Might have come to that," he admitted, and he saw her wince a little.

"This is a strange country," she said, "a violent country."

119

"But you like it," Emmett smiled.

"Yes," she admitted.

"You don't miss England?"

The English girl shook her head, and her dark eyes were serious. "There is nothing in England for Clyde and myself," she said. "This is our home. Both of us like it here."

As if by agreement they were riding in the general direction of the streamer of smoke where Crown ranch lay. Riding with her, Emmett remembered Dean Brockton's remark with the insinuation that he was buying Bar B because he was interested in a neighbor. Bar B had two neighbors!

CHAPTER 10

Riding back to Crown ranch house, Emmett learned that Clyde Morrison had gone east to Cheyenne that morning, and would not be back for a few days. Hearing this, he grimaced but said nothing.

"Mr. Halloran seems to be very efficient," Pamela said. "He makes most of the decisions, as it is."

"Where did your brother meet up with Halloran?" Emmett asked her.

"In Omaha," Pamela explained. "Clyde was looking for land, and he needed advice. Mr. Halloran has been a great help to us."

Emmett nodded. They came in sight of Crown ranch, a big, rambling log affair with a number of smaller buildings. A new barn was going up in the rear, and the workmen turned to watch them as they rode up. Two men came out of the long, low bunkhouse to look at Emmett, and he sized them up immediately. There were other Crown riders down at the corral, and they bore the same label. Boyd Halloran had signed on a tough, hard-bitten crew, and he hadn't signed them just to work cattle. They were the same stamp as the rat-faced Pete Cooley, the new Hatchet hand.

Halloran, himself, came from the direction of

the barn, touched his black hat to Pamela and gave Emmett a searching look, nodding briefly. He signaled for a man to take Pamela's horse, and then he went on down to the corral, Emmett leaving Pamela on the porch.

Pamela said to him with a small grin before he rode away, "I would invite you in for a cup of tea if I didn't think your employer would object."

"Why would she object?" Emmett asked.

Pamela shrugged. "Is it customary for a ranch superintendent to have tea with a neighbor during working hours?"

"Some other time," Emmett smiled. "I won't forget it."

She was standing on the porch watching him as he rode on past the corral. Boyd Halloran was smoking a cigar, talking with a man there, and he turned again, looking at Emmett as he moved past. He said, "You make friends fast, Kane."

Emmett stopped the roan to look down at him. Halloran's turquoise eyes were smiling, but there was no mirth in them.

"I get along," Emmett agreed.

"Man needs friends in this part of the country," Halloran observed. Again, there was that veiled threat. "You were wise to sign up with Pine Tree."

"I'd have been wiser," Emmett told him, "to sign up with Crown brand. That right?"

Halloran shrugged. "Reckon we have enough hands," he said, "for what we're trying to do here."

Emmett rode on, leaving Crown ranch behind, and it was nearly dusk when he crossed Squaw Run and came up to Pine Tree.

Curly Evans watched him dismount in front of the stable and lead the roan to shelter. The little rider said, "You get everything done you set out to do?"

Emmett smiled at him. He wondered what Curly would say if he knew that Bar B was going to have a new owner very shortly. "Just about," he said.

"You figure on putting a guard down at the creek tonight?" Curly asked him.

"Every night," Emmett nodded. "I'll take the first watch."

"Miss Wilson's been kind of wondering where you're riding to," Curly told him.

"She ask?"

"She asked," Curly said.

"You don't know," Emmett told him.

Curly laughed. "Telling the truth," he grinned. "Ain't no business of mine where you been."

Emmett stripped the saddle from the roan. He said over his shoulder, "How far is Aspen City from here?"

"Twenty miles," Curly murmured, and then when Emmett didn't say anything he added thoughtfully, "You get around, Emmett."

The call came for supper, and they went over to the ranch house. Madge Wilson gave Emmett a sharp look as he followed Ben Adamson, Howlett and Curly Evans into the room.

There was little talk at the supper table. The three Pine Tree hands ate rapidly, and when they were finished they rose to go. Emmett was reaching for his hat when Madge spoke.

"Will you stay a few minutes, Emmett?"

Emmett nodded. He felt in his shirt pocket for a cigar, discovered that he didn't have one, and then Madge pointed to a box she kept on the table for visitors. Emmett took a cigar from the box and put it in his mouth. She watched him as he touched a match to it, and then sat down in the chair opposite her.

"You've been riding," she said, and he nodded, wondering if she were the kind of woman who insisted upon knowing every step her foreman took. He offered her no information, letting her know that he didn't intend to give a daily report of his activities.

She went off on a new tack, and said, "You think there'll be more attempts to run stock into the valley?"

Emmett shrugged. "Figure Hatchet had enough," he said. "Crown won't—not Morrison anyway. That leaves Brockton, and he can move in any time, with permission."

"You don't think Crown will give us any trouble?" Madge murmured.

"No," Emmett told her, and then he remembered

that Clyde Morrison was away, leaving Halloran in complete charge. He didn't think, though, that Halloran would have the nerve to attempt a forcible entry into Vermilion Valley while Morrison was gone.

There was a knock on the door, and then Curly Evans poked his head into the room. He said, "Hamp Freeman's coming up."

Emmett nodded. He'd been expecting a visit from the sheriff with some questions regarding Lee Ransom's death. They'd probably gotten Ransom's body into town in the late afternoon, and Freeman had had his supper before riding out to Pine Tree.

The sheriff of Elkhorn came into the room a minute or two later, his round face flushed because it had turned cold again with the sun gone. Freeman took off his hat, revealing his thin brown hair, parted exactly in the middle.

"Sit down, Sheriff," Madge invited.

Freeman sat down with his hat on his knees. He looked at Emmett, frowned, and said, "So you got yourself another man."

Emmett just looked at him and puffed on the cigar. He didn't like the way Hamp Freeman was putting it, and his silence was an indication of this.

"We found Ransom," Freeman growled, "and we got the body back to town. What's your side of it, Kane?"

Emmett nodded toward Madge Wilson. He said, "She'll tell you. I'm new in these parts."

Madge Wilson told briefly of the attack on the road, and of Emmett's going after the killer, riding her horse.

When she'd finished Hamp Freeman drummed with his fingers on the top of his hat for a few moments, and then he said to Emmett, "You followed Ransom out to the line camp where we found him?"

Emmett nodded.

"Sure you didn't make any mistakes?" Freeman asked him.

"What kind of mistakes?" Emmett countered.

"You had the right man when you found him in the cabin?" Freeman persisted. "You didn't lose his trail?"

Emmett smiled mirthlessly. "I didn't lose his trail," he said.

"Then you found Ransom in the cabin and you shot him."

Emmett took the cigar out of his mouth and looked at it. "I let him pull a gun first," he said.

"Gun wasn't used," Freeman said.

Emmett looked at the chubby man steadily. "Ransom was a mite slow with his lead," he said.

Freeman frowned at that. He put his hat on his head and then remembered Madge Wilson's presence and took it off again. He said, "Asking routine questions; that's my job."

"You'll have another pretty soon," Emmett said.

Hamp Freeman licked his lips. "How's that?" he asked.

"New Hatchet hand by the name of Pete Cooley," Emmett said. "Pulled a gun on me this afternoon so that Trev Wharton could work me over with a lead pipe. You tell Cooley to get the hell out of these parts or he'll be dead the next time we meet."

This was news to Madge Wilson, too, and Emmett saw her look at him quickly. Sheriff Freeman said sullenly, "Getting to be a hell of a town when a stranger can make a law saying who stays and who don't stay around. There's law and order in Elkhorn, Kane."

Emmett smiled at him. "Trev Wharton tried to work on me this afternoon with a lead pipe. This damned Cooley held a gun on me. What are you going to do about it, Sheriff?"

"You got proof?" Freeman growled.

"Ask Miss Morrison," Emmett said, and again he felt Madge Wilson's eyes on him, not too friendly now.

Freeman hadn't expected this, and he was disconcerted for the moment. "I'll look up Wharton," he said gruffly.

"Cooley's the man I'm after," Emmett observed. "Cooley pulled a gun on me."

"All right," Freeman snapped. "I'll see Cooley, too."

"That was what I asked you to do in the first place," Emmett said softly.

Hamp Freeman left in a bad humor, and when he'd gone Madge said, "You had an exciting afternoon. I suppose you had tea with Miss Morrison?"

"She invited me," Emmett said. "I didn't accept."

Madge hesitated for a moment, and then she said, "Why not?"

Emmett smiled. "Part of my job to answer a question like that?" he murmured.

The girl reddened a little. "All right," she said. "It's none of my business, but I didn't know you were that friendly with Miss Morrison." Emmett didn't say anything to that, and she knew again that he was displeased. She said immediately, "I'm sorry, Emmett, but this whole business is getting on my nerves. It's the waiting, expecting almost any night to find strange stock in the valley, and knowing that it will take guns to get them out."

"Why don't you marry Brockton," Emmett said, "and let a man do the worrying for you?"

He thought of Brockton running away, then, taking all he could get for his range. The man wasn't big enough to side the girl everyone thought he intended to marry.

Madge Wilson looked down at her hands, and her blue eyes were sober. "What do you think of Dean?" she asked.

"He's not your kind of man," Emmett told her. "You know it, too."

She did know it. He saw that in her eyes when she looked at him, and he knew, also, that if he wanted to he could take Brockton's place this moment. A day or two before, this revelation would have pleased him; but he wasn't sure now. He wanted to know more about this girl rancher who could be either soft or hard, and who never seemed to be the same from one day to the next. At this moment, with the lamplight playing upon her smooth face and illuminating her nut-brown hair, she was soft and alluring. Emmett felt his breath coming faster.

"What kind of man is my man?" Madge smiled at him. "You seem to know me."

"I don't know you," Emmett shook his head. "That's the trouble."

"Am I so hard to know?" Madge said softly, and he was amazed at how quickly she was dismissing Dean Brockton.

"I'll find out, some day," Emmett told her, and then he left. When he was outside he wished that he hadn't left, and he was in bad humor.

When he entered the bunkhouse Curly Evans said to him, "That damned Freeman rode away from here like he wasn't too happy about something."

Emmett just shrugged. He finished his cigar, sitting down on the edge of his bunk, and then without a word to the other men he put on his jacket, threw a saddle on one of the spare horses in the barn, and rode out to the line shack at Squaw Run.

His watch till midnight was a quiet one. He got the fire going in the shack, and sat in front of it, warming himself, as the night had turned quite cold. Then he walked up and down along the north bank of the creek, listening for sounds. The stars were very bright, glittering in the dark heavens. There was no moon, but in the starlight he could make out the dim ramparts surrounding Vermilion Valley behind him.

When Dave Howlett came out to relieve him he had the fire going strongly in the shack. The veteran rider said, "Could be a heap of foolishness sitting out here, Emmett, but you never know. Rather stop 'em here than have to run 'em out once they're in."

Emmett nodded. "Who do you figure will make the try, Dave?" he asked.

Howlett shrugged as he held his hands toward the flames. "Reckon I don't like it that Morrison left. That Boyd Halloran's a bad one. He could make trouble for us."

"We'll watch him," Emmett agreed.

He went back to Pine Tree, slept until a little before dawn, and then stepped into the kitchen for a quick breakfast before riding out. The Indian woman had hot coffee on the stove, and she asked no questions.

Saddling the roan, Emmett rode away just as the

130

first yellow light was coming into the sky. It was very cold at this hour, but the day promised to be clear.

Curly Evans had the morning watch at the shack, and as Emmett rode up, the little rider came out of the shack to look at him.

"Going up to Aspen City, are you?" he said.

"Due north?" Emmett asked.

"Swing up over that hogback," Curly told him. "You'll run into the old stage road on the other side. Follow your nose into Aspen. Ain't much up there, though. Smaller than Elkhorn."

"I'll see it," Emmett smiled.

"Hell of a ride, just to look at nothing," Curly murmured. "You want me to tell Miss Wilson anything?"

Emmett shook his head. "She'll know I'm gone," he said. "I should be back by dark."

"Twenty miles each way," Curly said skeptically. "Maybe you will and maybe you won't, depending on the weather."

Emmett crossed Squaw Run, rode due east and over the hogback Curly Evans had nodded to, and picked up the stage road on the other side. The stage road, he discovered, was a continuation of the old trace which led out to Vermilion Valley from Elkhorn. The stage company had gone out of business when the railroad reached Elkhorn, and the road was used only by occasional freight wagons.

There were no fresh tracks in the road, and Emmett assumed that either he'd started out earlier than Dean Brockton, or Brockton was taking a different route up to Aspen City. The latter explanation seemed the more logical. Brockton would expect him to take the stage road, not knowing the country too well; while Brockton would ride up over a more direct route so that they wouldn't be seen together by any stray riders.

The sun was out full when he hit the stage road, but it didn't remain out very long. Gray clouds filled up the northern sky, and Emmett wondered if they were snow clouds. It didn't seem cold enough to snow, but the weather seemed to change rapidly in this northern range country.

At noon, having seen no one on the road, he pulled off at one of the old stage stations, built himself a small fire inside the tumble-down stone corral, and fried a few strips of bacon. He'd dropped some biscuits into his saddlebags before starting out that morning, and this, with some cold water from the stream behind the corral, made his lunch.

When he pushed on again the whole sky was overcast, and a chill wind was whipping down from the north. He wondered if that meant a blizzard, the first one of this early winter season. He'd heard them talking about blizzards back in Elkhorn. It wouldn't be pleasant to be out in one.

It was past two o'clock in the afternoon when

he topped a rise in the road and saw the little town of Aspen City nestled in the valley below, a single, straggling main street, smoke whipping up into the air from every chimney, a few horses and buckboards standing in front of the stores.

He rode in with his leather jacket buttoned tight around his neck, dismounting in front of the Longhorn Saloon at the other end of town. There were three other saloons in Aspen, the Longhorn being the smallest, and he smiled a little, considering Dean Brockton's caution. Even here, some distance from Elkhorn, he was afraid they would be seen together. He wondered if Brockton would suggest that they go to the lawyer's office separately.

There were no horses out in front of the Longhorn, and he expected to find the saloon empty at this hour; but there were two men at the bar, and both of them turned to look at him when they heard the door open.

One of the men Emmett did not know, a slim, thin-shouldered, hawk-faced man of dark complexion, with black Indian eyes. The other man was Boyd Halloran, ramrod of Crown.

CHAPTER 11

Emmett's face was expressionless, his gray eyes bleak, as he came forward to the bar, taking a position about six feet from the hawk-faced man. Halloran was on the other side of the man, a beer glass in his hand, a half-smile on his face.

The bartender came toward Emmett from the other end of the bar, where he'd been reading an old newspaper. Emmett pointed to a bottle on the shelf, and the bartender got it down, slid a shot glass in front of him, and then moved back to his newspaper again. Not a word had been spoken.

Boyd Halloran broke the silence in the room. He said casually, "You get around, Kane."

Emmett poured himself a drink, lifted the glass to look at it, and said, "I like to ride."

He wondered if Dean Brockton had told Halloran, and if this were a trap here in Aspen City. If Brockton hadn't tipped off Halloran, and Halloran had learned some other way, or suspected their intentions, then Brockton was riding into Aspen any moment now, and running into the one man he didn't want to see. He had to grin, thinking of the expression on Brockton's face when he walked into this saloon and saw Halloran at the bar.

He could tell nothing from Halloran's face. The big, blond man with the wide shoulders may have had a man watching him all the time once he suspected him of dealing with Dean Brockton, and when he rode north toward Aspen City, Halloran, going by a more direct route overland, could have beaten him to the little cowtown.

The dark man with Halloran was another Pete Cooley, possibly with Indian blood in him. He carried a pearl-handled Colt on his hip, and the holster was smooth and worn.

"Maybe," Halloran smiled, "you're looking for Pine Tree strays up this way, Kane."

Emmett smiled at him. He downed his drink, put the glass down and a coin on the bar. He wasn't sure how much Halloran knew or suspected, and he didn't intend to give the man any information. Possibly Halloran did not even know Brockton was riding up this way, and was fishing for information. "You had a long ride, Halloran, for a glass of beer," he commented.

"I like beer." Boyd Halloran grinned. He watched Emmett walking toward the door, and then he looked at the hawk-faced man with him.

Emmett closed the door behind him and stood on the porch outside for a moment, watching the first few flakes of snow beginning to fall. It had become colder, and the wind was blowing down the street, rattling signs on buildings.

Knowing he was being watched from inside, Emmett stepped down to the tie-rack, untied the roan, and then walked up the street in the direction of a livery stable he'd noticed on the way in. He spotted the office of the town's only lawyer, up on the second floor above a dry goods store. The name was on the window: "Jonas C. Flynn, Attorney at Law."

He noted the location of the building, the alley leading up from the building, and the side door off the alley. He did this as he walked the roan up the street, eventually tying the animal out in front of the big general store in town. He'd stopped less than fifty yards from the Longhorn Saloon, in which Halloran and his companion still waited, watching him through the closed door window.

Looking south down the street as he went under the tie-rack and up on the walk, he noticed that there were no riders coming in. If Dean Brockton were innocent of any double-dealing, he was still on his way to Aspen City, and he had to be intercepted before he rode into view. Emmett decided to gamble on the possibility that Brockton had not told Halloran, and was still riding north to the meeting with him in the Longhorn Saloon.

The snow was coming thicker as Emmett stepped into the store, finding the proprietor talking with a woman customer over near the cloth counter. He had a bolt of blue and white cloth on the counter, and Emmett was quite sure they'd be busy over there for a few minutes as the woman made up her mind about the cloth.

He moved around looking at various items, until

he was at the rear of the room; and then noting that neither the proprietor nor the customer were looking his way, he stepped to the door, opened it, and went out into the rear yard.

There was a wagon shed back here with two buckboards under it, and an outhouse next to the shed. Emmett crossed the yard quickly, and then moved down behind the row of buildings facing the street. He went across vacant, litter-strewn lots.

When he reached the last house on the street, he continued on, walking parallel with the stage road until he was several hundred yards from town, and he could no longer see the town because of the falling snow, which was coming thick and wet. He stood under a clump of cottonwoods which afforded some small shelter, and he watched the road, the thought still persisting that Dean Brockton hadn't told Halloran, and was still headed for Aspen City and the extra money he would receive for selling his ranch to Emmett Kane.

Twenty minutes passed, and then thirty, and the flat crown of Emmett's hat held half an inch of snow before a rider came out of the storm, head bent to the wind. Emmett recognized Brockton's black leather jacket, and he stepped from the cottonwood grove, calling Brockton's name.

Brockton pulled off the road. He looked at Emmett curiously, and Emmett said,

137

"Figured I'd meet you outside of town and we'd walk in down a back alley. Better if you're not seen in this town except by the lawyer."

Brockton nodded in agreement. "Where's your horse?" he asked.

"Left him back in town," Emmett explained. "You can follow me in."

He walked on ahead, turning off the road again, and coming in behind the line of buildings on the main street. Once he glanced back to see if Brockton was coming along. The Bar B owner was a dozen yards behind him, the horse walking slowly through the snow, making little sound. There was a faint smile on Emmett's face as he swung around again, and he wondered how quickly Brockton would get out of here if he knew Boyd Halloran and a paid gunhand were in Aspen City.

When they reached the alley where he'd seen the side door, Emmett stopped, signaled for Brockton to dismount. They went down the alley on foot and stepped in through the doorway of the building. They shook the snow from their clothing as they stood on the lower floor landing, and then started up the stairs toward the office of Jonas Flynn, the lawyer.

Brockton said, "You have that bank draft, Kane?"

"I have it."

The heavy odor of cigar smoke lay in the corridor as they mounted the stairs, and the lawyer's office door was open. He was an enormously fat man, bulging out over the sides of the chair behind the rolltop desk.

Waving them to chairs in the room he boomed, "What can I do for you, gentlemen?"

Emmett took the chair by the window over-looking the street. He accepted a cigar from the box Jonas Flynn pushed toward him, and put it in his mouth. As he was touching a match to it, he looked down into the street. He could see his roan horse still tied up in front of the general store across the road, and then he saw Boyd Halloran and his rider come out of the store. Halloran threw a half-smoked cigar savagely into the gutter, and he stood there with his hands jammed in the pockets of his heavy woolen jacket, staring up and down the street. Evidently, they'd gotten tired of waiting for him to come out of the store and had walked up to investigate. Halloran had to figure out where he'd gone now, and he was not pleased that he'd been given the slip.

Jonas Flynn was saying, "Transfer of title? You have the deed to your property with you, Mr. Brockton?"

The lawyer went through the papers rapidly, humming a soft tune. Then he said to Emmett, "You are prepared to pay cash, sir?"

Emmett handed him the bank draft without a word, and the fat man whistled a little.

"We'll take it over to the bank," he said, "after we've made out the papers."

Emmett leaned back in the chair, his hat on his knee. "Where is the bank?" he asked.

"Next building," Flynn told him. "Aspen National Bank."

Emmett hadn't noticed it riding into town, and he assumed the bank was in a store. It wouldn't be very big. He sat hunched in the chair, watching the lawyer draw up new legal papers, his pen scratching busily.

When he'd finished he stood up and said, "We'll get you your money, Mr. Brockton, before we sign the papers."

Emmett put his hat on. He said, "Brockton can wait here till we get back."

Surprise came into Dean Brockton's brown eyes, and he looked up at Emmett quickly.

"Better," Emmett said, and Brockton slowly nodded in agreement.

Jonas Flynn looked from one man to the other, and then shrugged. Emmett followed him downstairs to the front door of the building. He stopped at the door and said to the lawyer, "You go on ahead. I want a word with Brockton."

Flynn nodded. "Don't be long," he said, and went out into the street.

Emmett waited a moment, and then opened the door. He looked up and down the street before stepping out, and he caught a glimpse of Halloran at the far end, coming out of a livery stable alley. He waited until Halloran's back was turned, and then he walked quickly up to the next building and stepped inside. The snow lay an inch deep on the board walk now, and he could see the big footprints left by the lawyer.

It took a matter of minutes to have a check made out to Brockton's order, and the remainder of the money changed in to another bank draft in Emmett's name.

They came out of the bank, Emmett pausing again to look up and down the street before following the lawyer back to his office. He didn't see Boyd Halloran at all this time, and he was smiling a little as he went up the stairs to Flynn's office.

Brockton was still sitting in the same chair, smoking his cigar. He looked at the check as Emmett placed it on the desk top, and licked his lips nervously.

Jonas Flynn called the storekeeper from below to witness their signatures, and then Brockton picked up his check. Emmett stuffed the thick envelope into his jacket pocket, and paid the lawyer for his services. The deal was consummated.

"You are in business, Mr. Kane." Jonas Flynn smiled. "Good luck."

"Might need it," Emmett murmured, and he smiled at Dean Brockton.

They went down the stairs together, both of them still smoking Flynn's cigars, and when they reached the bottom landing Brockton said, "You won't come near Bar B until I've had a chance to pack up a few things and clear out?"

Emmett nodded. "A week should be enough," he agreed. As Brockton was about to open the side door which led into the alley, Emmett said to him, "Careful riding back."

"I aim to be careful," Brockton said absently.

"Friend of yours in town," Emmett went on, and Brockton stopped and turned around.

"Who?"

"Boyd Halloran," Emmett said, "out on the main street."

Dean Brockton didn't say anything. He just looked at Emmett, the fear and the dislike in his eyes, and Emmett was not sure which was the stronger.

"All right," Brockton almost whispered. "All right, Kane."

"You've got nothing to worry about," Emmett told him. "Halloran doesn't even know you're here. You can ride out the way you came in, and be back at your place sometime after dark." He puffed on the cigar and added, "Might be safer in Aspen City, though, in this storm."

"I'm going on," Brockton said quickly. "You don't think Halloran will see me?"

"He's looking for me," Emmett told him.

"You could have told me," Brockton accused.

"Would you have come in?" Emmett countered.

Dean Brockton pulled up his jacket collar,

looked at Emmett, and then opened the door. He stood in the open doorway for some time, letting the snow and cold air come in as he watched the main street, and then suddenly he darted out, heading up the alley toward his horse.

Emmett was smiling as he walked on through the store to the street entrance and went out. He was crossing the road when he saw Halloran come out of a saloon a few doors down from the general store. Halloran saw him at the same instant and stopped in his tracks on the walk, the snow swirling about him.

Rubbing the flank of the roan, Emmett walked on, lifting a hand to Halloran as he went by, and stepping into the saloon. At the empty bar he had a straight whiskey to warm himself for the long, cold ride ahead, and then he came out again, feeling a little remorseful that he'd had to leave the roan out in the snow all this time.

He didn't see Halloran now, but he knew that Halloran was watching him, and he was quite sure that when he started to ride back to Pine Tree ranch Halloran and his man would be behind him. What they would try to do he did not know. Halloran had learned exactly nothing by following him to Aspen City, even though he was positive Emmett Kane had been up to something.

Climbing into the saddle, Emmett turned the roan south. He didn't turn to look back until he'd left the last building far behind, and the roan was moving along the stage road at a leisurely pace, knowing it had a long distance to go.

He didn't see anything when he turned his head. The snowflakes swirled around him, and he couldn't see more than fifty or seventy-five yards in any direction. He could imagine Dean Brockton far ahead of him, driving through the snow with a clammy fear inside him, and he hoped nothing happened to the man for avoiding the stage road and cutting across country in a storm like this. In two hours it would be dark.

A mile out of Aspen City, Emmett turned off the road, riding the roan into a thin scattering of fir trees on a slope. He dismounted, tied the horse to a tree, and then walked up and down to keep himself warm, at the same time watching the road. He noticed that the tracks the roan had made coming off the road were being obliterated by the driving snow, and in a few moments would be gone altogether.

Screened behind the trees, he watched the road. Soon he saw a rider coming out of the veil of flying snow, and recognized Boyd Halloran's chestnut horse. Halloran was alone.

CHAPTER 12

Watching Halloran ride up, Emmett frowned a little. He waited for the hawk-faced man to come along behind Halloran, but Halloran rode by, big shoulders hunched, the chestnut's tail to the driving snow. No one followed.

When Halloran had gone on out of sight, Emmett waited for fully ten minutes, trying to make up his mind. Possibly Halloran had left his man back in Aspen City and was returning to Crown ranch alone. On the other hand, Halloran may have had the hawk-faced man string along behind him, expecting that Emmett Kane would be watching for them and do exactly as he was doing now.

With Halloran up ahead of him, and the gunman coming behind, it meant that Emmett was caught in a pocket. In a storm like this, and in a country completely strange to him, it would be foolish to leave the road. Halloran knew that.

Emmett couldn't wait too long here, either, if he didn't want to be caught in this storm all night. He'd heard that men sometimes froze to death in the saddle when the temperature dropped low enough and deep snow had made it impossible for their horses to break through. If he waited, and the hawk-faced man wasn't coming behind, he was waiting in vain.

Another fifteen minutes passed, and then Emmett stepped into the saddle, took the roan back into the road and followed Halloran. The fact that Halloran may have stepped off the road, also, and was lying in ambush for him at this moment was another disquieting factor, and after moving on for nearly half an hour, watching every clump of dark rock, he decided that he had enough of it. He had to watch his backtrail, too, expecting any moment to see the Crown gunhand riding out of the snow, flame spurting from the muzzle of his gun.

Drawing off the road again, Emmett waited, and then lifting his gun from the holster he fired once, hesitated, and then fired twice more in rapid succession. He pulled back behind a fringe of willows and waited, wondering what this bait would bring.

The man behind or the man in front of him would certainly assume that the other had caught up with his quarry, and would come running to get in on the fight.

Inserting fresh cartridges into the gun cylinder, Emmett waited. The first rider appeared from the direction of Aspen City, riding hard through the snow on a black horse with four white stockings. Emmett saw the gun in the hand of the hawk-faced man as he tore through the snow. Lifting his gun, he sent a shot over his head.

The rider pulled up instantly, jerking the black's head around. His gun winked orange in the falling snow, but he shot hastily, his horse moving under him, and he missed. He turned his horse quickly and headed back toward Aspen City. Emmett knew he'd have no more trouble from him.

Mounting the roan again, Emmett rode straight forward, the gun within easy reach of his right hand. The odds were even now—one man against one, and he didn't think Halloran cared too much for these odds—not that Halloran was afraid of him. Halloran had big plans, and he would not care to die under the gun of a drifting rider who'd signed on with Pine Tree. There was a good chance that Halloran would go straight on to Crown ranch and let him alone this time.

He rode on for an hour, and then another hour as the light left the sky and the snow deepened in the road. Once he stopped to breathe the roan, and he squatted under some pine trees off the road, smoking a cigarette, his back to the snow, coat collar turned up and hatbrim low.

He was positive that Halloran had had no liking for a fight on an afternoon like this, and had kept moving ahead. His fight now was not against the Crown foreman, but against the weather. Pine Tree ranch was still several hours away. It was nightfall. The snow was piling up, seeming to increase in intensity. If he were to stray from the stage road in the dark he would have a hard time reaching Vermilion Valley, if he reached it at all.

He rode forward again, giving the animal free rein, hoping that the horse would be able to follow the natural contours of the road in the darkness better than he. The wind seemed to have veered around from the north to the northwest, making it harder going. He began to feel the chill through the leather jacket and the woolen sweater he'd put on that morning. The right side of his face where the wind and the snow hit became numb, and he had to take off one glove and rub the cheek vigorously.

Several times the roan stumbled over the uneven ground, and again Emmett pulled up to give the animal a rest. The snow on the ground was at least six inches deep now, and much deeper where it had drifted. Once going across a fording place the roan had plunged through the ice, the water coming nearly up to the stirrups, and had had to struggle out.

They'd been making slow progress, and he figured that Vermilion Valley still lay another three hours ahead of him. He had to stamp up and down in the snow for a few minutes to bring the circulation back into his feet, and he realized then that they had to stop and find shelter for the night.

The old stage station at which he'd had lunch that noon would have provided some shelter, but he was considerably beyond that point now, and it would have been foolish to attempt to ride back.

He remembered, then, that he'd passed another stage station on his left that morning as he rode up from Vermilion Valley. This station had been small, probably a swing station on the old line. There had been a tumble-down shack with a few horse sheds behind it. The shack, if he could find it, would provide shelter for the night, and also firewood for a fire.

Rising into the saddle, he pushed forward again, peering through the darkness now, not even sure he was still on the stage road. The roan plodded along, breathing heavily, stumbling through the drifts. Once they moved up to the top of a rise where the snow had been blown clear by the wind, and Emmett could make out the faint wagon ruts below him, and he knew they were still on the stage road.

He remembered this rise. The swing station was on the other side of it in a little hollow. There was a stand of timber leading up the grade, and as Emmett went down he could make out the trees as a thick wall on his right. When he came to the edge of the wall he turned the roan off the road, and then the wall of the shack loomed up in front of him.

Stiffly he dismounted, and led the horse around to the lee side of the shack out of the driving snow, and then he felt his way inside, stumbling over fallen boards. The door came down as he pried it open, landing with a bang inside.

Stepping in out of the wind, he took off his gloves, blew on his hands until he was able to work the fingers properly, and then struck a match. The room was very small, barely large enough for the two bunks, and a table and chairs. The bunks were broken down, and the table lay in one corner, two of the legs broken from it.

There was a fireplace, and Emmett moved toward this before his match burned out. He struck another match, located a few old newspapers he found in one corner of the room and shoved them into the fireplace. He touched the match to the paper, and when the paper started to burn he had light by which he could search for wood.

One side of the shack had fallen in, and there were loose boards here. Wrenching several of them free, he stood them against the door post and stamped on them with his boot, breaking the wood into pieces and feeding the smaller pieces into the flames.

In a few minutes he had a good fire going, and there was heat in the room even though the south wall, away from the wind, was down. He broke up more wood, heavier now, using the table and the broken-down bunks, and then he went outside to lead the horse in through the door.

Stripping off the saddle he rubbed the animal down as best he could with the dry portion of the saddle blanket, and then he took a few quarts of oats out of the saddle bag and fed him.

Rummaging around inside the shack he found a battered tin bucket. Then he located the frozen stream fifteen yards from the shack, and brushing away the snow, kicked a hole into the ice, and filled the bucket. He carried it back, and the horse drank.

Before sitting down to fry the few pieces of bacon he had remaining from his dinner that day, Emmett closed the door by standing it in the entrance and wedging a board against it. There was one window in the shack, partially exposed to the storm, and snow was drifting in. He closed this by draping a few old burlap bags across the opening.

The fire was burning strongly in the fireplace now, and he felt fairly comfortable as he squatted in front of the flames, holding his strips of bacon on the tip of his knife.

He had one biscuit remaining from his dinner, and he ate that with the bacon, washing it down again with cold water, and the meal, though meager, took the edge off his hunger.

After breaking up more wood for the fire during the night, he lay down on the blanket and slept soundly until the morning.

He was awakened by the cold, and he found that his fire was nearly out. Piling on more wood, he soon had it burning high again, and then he stepped to the door, thrust it aside, and looked out.

The snow had stopped, but a blanket of white

covered the land. It was nearly a foot deep, weighing down the branches of trees and piled up on the roof of the shack, making it sag dangerously.

He led the roan out of the shack, saddled, and rode back to the stage road. It was tough going for the horse, plunging through occasional drifts, and by noon when they reached the hogback and turned in toward Vermilion Valley, the animal was almost done in.

Crossing Squaw Run, Emmett saw smoke drifting up into the gray winter sky from the direction of Dean Brockton's ranch, and he knew that Brockton had gotten through safely. He remembered that now he was riding on his own range, and that he had stock to look after. As a man who'd never owned land, but plenty of cattle on the hoof, it gave him a strange feeling. He wondered what Madge Wilson would say when she learned of it.

Curly Evans came out of the barn to look at him as he rode up, unshaven, dirty from the night in the shack, and with a hungry look in his eyes.

Curly scratched his chin and said, "Reckon you run into something, Emmett. I'll take care of the horse. You get into the kitchen and put some hot coffee into your belly."

"Rub him down," Emmett said as Curly was leading the roan into the stable.

"I know what a horse needs," Curly said.

Emmett stepped into the kitchen through the back door. He found the Indian woman getting dinner, and he sat down at the table. She brought him the coffee pot and put it down in front of him with a cup, and then she filled up a huge platter with bacon and eggs.

The eggs were still sizzling when Madge Wilson came into the room. He'd seen her through the kitchen window talking with Dave Howlett, who'd been out in the snow, and just ridden in.

The snow in Vermilion Valley was less than six inches deep. He'd noticed that when he came across Squaw Run. The high mountains to the north, forming a semicircle around the valley, had cut off much of the snow.

Madge came over and stood on the other side of the table, looking down at him. Her face was white with anger, and her blue eyes hard. She said slowly, "You've been away a long time, Emmett."

"Had a little business in Aspen," Emmett explained. "Caught in that storm on the way back. I had to hole up in one of the old stage stations."

Madge bit her lips. "Was your business Pine Tree business?" she asked.

Emmett looked at her. "No," he admitted.

"Pine Tree is paying your wages."

Emmett put both hands flat on the tabletop. "You asking me to ride off?" he said.

Madge sat down on the other side of the table. The Indian woman brought the platter of bacon and eggs, and another plate full of biscuits. Emmett sat there, looking across the table, and Madge said to him wearily, "Go ahead and eat."

He knew then that something was wrong, and it was more than just his riding off for a whole day on his own business. He waited for her to speak as he started to eat, and she said,

"I'm not trying to keep your nose to the grindstone for the money I pay you, but I did hire you to keep neighboring stock out of this valley."

Emmett stopped eating. "Some come in last night?" he asked.

"Dave Howlett counted nearly two thousand head this morning. They were run across last night in the storm. We couldn't even try to stop them."

Emmett sipped his coffee. "Crown?" he asked.

"Mostly Crown stock," Madge nodded; "some Hatchet."

Emmett's face was expressionless. "You know Morrison went to Cheyenne?"

"I'd heard it," Madge nodded. "I'm sure this was Halloran, on his own."

Emmett ate slowly, not tasting the food now. Halloran had gone on yesterday afternoon, beating his way back to Crown ranch, and then he rounded up his riders, and in the middle of the storm picked up whatever stock he could find and pushed them across Squaw Run.

"Who was out at the shack last night?" Emmett wanted to know.

"Ben," Madge told him. "There wasn't anything we could do. They kept coming across."

"Riders behind them?"

"We heard shots."

Emmett looked at her steadily. "Why do you think Halloran went ahead with this while Morrison was gone?"

Madge shrugged. "Maybe he thinks he's bigger than his job," she said. "Maybe he has his own reasons."

"I'll find out," Emmett murmured. "Today."

"You're going over there?"

Emmett smiled a little. "What did you expect me to do?" he said. "I saw the Whartons."

"Halloran isn't Trev Wharton," Madge murmured, and he noticed that she didn't tell him not to go. "I intend to see Hamp Freeman," she said.

Emmett just smiled and went on eating.

"If there's law in this part of the country," Madge said grimly, "it should be on our side."

"You think Freeman will buck Boyd Halloran?"

She knew better than that, and he could see it in her eyes. Freeman was only talk. Freeman would protest to Clyde Morrison when he returned so that the Englishman would become a little more disgusted with his attempt at ranching in this north country, and pull out, leaving everything to Halloran—Crown, Bar B, and Vermilion Valley after Halloran had broken Pine Tree by taking over Brockton's Bar B. That had been Halloran's

155

purpose in running stock into the valley. He was to keep the Englishman always in a state of unrest until ranching here became odious to him.

"I'll have the boys start rounding up Crown stock," Emmett said, "as soon as we come back."

"I don't want any trouble," Madge protested mildly.

"Halloran started the trouble," Emmett observed, and he went on eating.

Madge left him, and when he'd finished he went out to the barn, where Curly Evans was currying the roan. Ben Adamson and Dave Howlett were there, and they eyed him curiously as he came in.

Emmett said, "Saddle up."

Curly Evans grinned and put the brush down. "Where we going?" he asked.

"We'll find out what Crown stock is doing in Vermilion Valley," Emmett told him. He picked out a bay animal in the stable and threw his saddle across its back. He said to Dave Howlett without looking at him, "Maybe better for you to stay here, Dave. Look after things."

"What for?" Howlett asked quietly.

Emmett tightened the cinch. "Reckon you haven't done any shooting lately, Dave."

"Reckon I ain't forgot how," Dave told him. "I'll ride, Emmett. Pine Tree is my brand."

"We gonna shoot up Crown?" Ben Adamson asked.

"Mightn't come to shooting," Emmett said, "this time."

"Getting sick of palaver," Curly Evans grunted. "We talk, and that damn Halloran acts."

"It could be," Emmett murmured, "that he went too far this time." He was remembering that Halloran had probably sent Lee Ransom after him, and yesterday Halloran had set another killer on his trail. How far did Halloran think he could be pushed?

CHAPTER 13

The four of them crossed Squaw Run on the ice, the horses moving gingerly. A sickly sun was trying to break through a wall of gray cloud. The wind still came from the northwest, and while there was no more snow in it for the time being, it was cold—very cold.

They were on Bar B range now, but Emmett saw no stock, and when he mentioned this fact to Curly Evans, Curly said laconically, "Bar B stuff drifts into the valley at the first sign of snow. They been doing it for years. He ain't got nothing to worry about, that Brockton."

They were skirting Brockton's ranch house, and the three Pine Tree hands assumed they would ride past it when Emmett turned his bay horse directly toward the house.

Curly Evans said in surprise, "He going with us?"

Emmett smiled. "Would he go?" he asked softly.

"Not unless he was dragged," Curly grinned.

"It's a social visit," Emmett explained, and he dismounted at the door, the three Pine Tree riders remaining in the saddles.

Dean Brockton came out, and Emmett pointed to the door, following the man inside. He said, when Brockton had closed the door behind him, "You got through all right?"

"What about you?" Brockton wanted to know, "and Halloran?"

"You see me," Emmett smiled.

"Halloran's dead?"

"You're not that lucky," Emmett grinned. "He's back at Crown ranch, and last night he ran two thousand head of beef into Vermilion Valley. You hear them go by?"

"I was sleeping," Brockton scowled. "I came in dead tired after that ride."

"And you weren't listening very hard."

"Why should I listen?" Brockton flared. "I'm pulling out of here today."

"Sooner the better," Emmett nodded.

Brockton licked his lips. "Halloran doesn't know?" he asked. "You haven't seen him?"

"No," Emmett said. "You're safe, but don't waste any time."

"If there's a train going out tonight," Brockton said, "I'll be on it, and then to hell with everybody."

"You saying good-bye to Miss Wilson?"

"That's my business," Dean Brockton snapped.

Emmett shrugged. "I won't tell her until you're gone," he said, "if that's the way you want it."

"I didn't say I wanted it any way."

"I know how you want it," Emmett told him. He turned toward the door again, and when he spoke this time there was almost pity in his voice. Dean Brockton was a weak man. Maybe he couldn't help being weak. He said, "Good luck, Brockton. You might need it, even in the East."

Brockton had nothing to say as Emmett closed the door behind him. As the four Pine Tree men rode away, Curly Evans spoke.

"He didn't offer to come along, Emmett?"

"No," Emmett said.

Curly shook his head contemptuously. "There's his stock finding shelter in Vermilion Valley," he said, "and Madge Wilson letting him do it, and never once does he lend a hand to keep the valley for her."

"Let him alone now," Emmett said. "It's tough for a man like that to live with himself."

"How would you like to be a woman and have to live with him?" Curly asked.

Emmett didn't say anything. He knew that that was over, but strangely enough it gave him no lift. Brockton was leaving the country, and Madge Wilson was free, and he should have been feeling elated. He'd saved Vermilion Valley for her, and she would be grateful to him for that. If he wanted, he was first in line now, but the thought left him cold. Possibly, after things settled down, after he'd had it out with Halloran, he would feel differently. He didn't know.

Riding toward Crown ranch he noticed how deep the snow was here, in comparison with the fall in the valley. Clumps of Crown stock stood around in the snow, pawing, trying to uncover the dried grass.

"Ain't bad yet," Curly said. "Wait'll we get a few more of these, Emmett, and it piles up. You'll see 'em dropping."

Emmett didn't say anything to that. They rode on until they came in sight of Crown ranch. The snow was trampled around the buildings, and men were shoveling paths from the stable to the corral and the house. As the Pine Tree riders rode up, the Crown shovelers stopped to watch them. A man came out of the bunkhouse, yawning, stretching himself, blinking. He was small, rat-faced, bulky in a heavy mackinaw and flat-crowned hat.

Curly Evans said softly, "Reckon Halloran's got himself a new rider, Emmett. That's Pete Cooley. He must of quit the Whartons."

Emmett had recognized the little gunman, too, and he remembered the promise he'd made to Sheriff Freeman. Cooley had pulled a gun on him, and Cooley had to answer for that.

Cooley watched them insolently as they dismounted, tying the horses to the corral posts. There were four Crown hands in sight, tough, hard-faced men. One of them spat in the snow as Emmett came up the path from the corral, the Pine Tree riders following him. To this man Emmett said, "Halloran around?"

"Ain't seen him." The Crown man scowled.

Pete Cooley stood with his back to the bunkhouse

wall, that same insolent smile on his face. He had a sliver of wood in his mouth as a toothpick, and he moved the sliver from side to side.

Emmett looked at him over the shoulder of the Crown rider, and said, "Changed brands, didn't you, Cooley?"

As he spoke he moved around the Crown man and came up to stand in front of the little gunhand, less than six feet away.

Cooley said, "What if I have?"

He had his gunbelt on, and his coat was open so that he could swing the gun into the clear without any trouble.

"You figure you're safer with a bigger outfit?"

Cooley pushed away from the wall, the smile gone from his face. He said softly, "You talk big, Kane." His amber snake's eyes slipped down to the gun on Emmett's hip. "You talk big," he said again.

"You pulled a gun on me the other day," Emmett said. "You don't forget that, Cooley?"

"I ain't forgot it," Cooley nodded. He was alert now, watching Emmett like a cat, his right hand at his side, nostrils dilating. He was a killer and he'd had his gunfights, and he waited now for Emmett to draw his gun.

Emmett took another step forward, making no attempt to go for his gun, and this move confused Cooley. In a gunfight a man did not walk forward. They were too close now, and he didn't like that part of it, either. It was almost impossible to miss at that distance.

Cooley couldn't back up, because the wall of the bunkhouse was directly behind him. He couldn't move to his right because the snow had been piled up there by the shovelers and was several feet high.

Deliberately, Emmett shifted his position so that Cooley couldn't break for the bunkhouse door, and the move cornered the little gunman. Out in the open, or in a spacious bar room, it would have been different, and he'd have gone for his gun. Here he was cornered like a rat, backed into this pocket almost as if he didn't have that big, dangerous weapon on his hip.

"All right," Cooley snarled. "All right, Kane."

He had to talk now to bolster his ebbing courage, and knowing this Emmett knew he had his man. Cooley should have drawn his gun when the thought came to him. Now it was too late.

Smiling, Emmett moved straight forward, making no attempt to go for his gun, and Cooley had been waiting for that gun hand to drop. When Emmett's hands closed on his forearms, he cursed, and made a futile attempt to wrench his gun loose from the holster.

He was no match for Emmett, who outweighed him by thirty or forty pounds and was a full six inches taller.

Emmett rammed him back against the wall of

the bunkhouse, shaking him up, and then he wrenched the gun from Cooley's holster and tossed it into the snowbank. The big Colt disappeared in the soft snow pile.

"That's all," Cooley yelped, and fear was in his voice. Without the gun, there was no strength in him.

Emmett pushed him back against the wall and then slapped his face with an open palm. Pete Cooley cursed and tried to break away, but Emmett pushed him back against the wall again, slapping Cooley's hands down, slapping him full across the face again and again, rocking him from side to side with the force of the blows.

The Crown hands leaned on their shovels, watching impassively, and the three Pine Tree riders watched them carefully. They made no attempt to interfere, and Emmett surmised that Cooley was not too popular in this bunkhouse, and they were quite willing to see him humiliated.

"I'll kill you!" Cooley screamed. "I'll kill you!"

He was almost sobbing. Emmett walked away from him then, putting his back to the man. For the moment he knew that he was safe, but Pete Cooley would come after him again—never face to face, but from the dark now, from an alley, and some day he would have to kill him as he'd killed Lee Ransom, who'd come in the dark.

The Crown riders were still leaning on their

shovels. They watched Pete Cooley stagger to his feet and lurch into the bunkhouse, and none of them moved.

Emmett said to the nearest man, "Halloran go into town?"

The Crown man looked across the corral, and when Emmett turned to look that way he saw three riders coming down the grade. The man in the lead rode a chestnut horse. It was Halloran.

Watching them swing around the corral, the horses kicking up snow, Emmett surmised that Halloran had been out looking over his stock which had not gone into Vermilion Valley. He had a cigar in his mouth as he came around the corral, and his hat was pulled low over his eyes.

"Here's the big one," Curly Evans said softly.

Emmett watched Halloran dismount and hand the reins to a man nearby. He came forward, his wide face expressionless. He wore a black and white checked woolen jacket. His face was smooth-shaven as usual, and flushed from the ride in the open.

He glanced toward the bunkhouse before speaking, and Emmett knew that he'd seen some of the scuffle with Pete Cooley.

"What's your business here, Kane?" he asked.

"A matter of two thousand head of Crown stock in Vermilion Valley," Emmett told him.

Boyd Halloran took the cigar from his mouth and looked at it. There was the faintest trace of humor in his voice and in his turquoise eyes when he spoke. He said, "Winter drift."

Emmett smiled. He said, "You have twenty-four hours to get them back across Squaw Run, Halloran."

"You're crazy," Halloran told him pleasantly. "Nobody in this part of the country bothers about winter drift stock until the spring."

"I bother about them," Emmett said.

"You're bothered about a lot of things," Halloran murmured.

"That's so," Emmett agreed.

"You're new to this country," Halloran went on, "and you don't know its customs. Until you do, my advice to you is to walk easy and talk easy, and keep to hell out of trouble."

"Should have given that advice to Lee Ransom," Emmett told him, "and your friend over in Aspen City."

Boyd Halloran said softly, "You talk in riddles, my friend."

"Here's a riddle for you," Emmett smiled. "Guess what'll happen to Crown stock if it's not out of Vermilion Valley by sundown tomorrow."

He heard Curly Evans chuckle softly behind him, and the red came to Halloran's face.

"Talk is no good with you, is it, Kane?" Halloran asked tersely.

"No good," Emmett agreed. "I'm not Dean Brockton."

Boyd Halloran tossed away the half-smoked cigar, and it sizzled out in a bank of soft snow. He said, "There are other ways besides talk." Then he took off his woolen jacket and draped it over one of the corral bars.

A Crown rider to Emmett's left said softly, "Here's one your size, Buck."

"You're next," Emmett informed him without even looking at the man. He watched Halloran unbuckle his gunbelt and place it across the jacket, and then he took off his own jacket, handing it to Curly Evans.

Halloran walked toward him deliberately, a thin smile on his face.

"You ever meet one your size, Kane?" he murmured.

"All sizes," Emmett told him, and then Halloran was on top of him, a big man, very swift, with the power of a bear, driving with his punches.

Instead of retreating, Emmett lowered his head and drove in, smashing both fists to the stomach, taking hard slashes to the face. As he tried to move forward, digging his boots into the mud and slush, he slipped and went down.

Halloran, still punching savagely and off balance, fell over him, and both men rolled in the snow, punching and kicking. Then they rolled away from each other and came up to their feet, Halloran's mouth open a little because the punches to the stomach had been hard.

Emmett tasted blood in his mouth. He moved in again, crouching a little, fists clenched, and then they met in another savage flurry, neither man willing to give ground.

They were still punching when they heard Pamela Morrison's voice, cool, but firm.

"That will be enough, gentlemen."

She had come down the shoveled lanes from the direction of the house, and she wore a black fur coat and a fur hat to match.

Emmett stepped back, feeling the little trickle of blood dripping down his chin. He looked at Halloran, who was breathing hard, his face taut.

"I think," Pamela observed, "that if there are any difficulties here we can discuss them without resort to force."

Halloran turned to pick up his gunbelt and jacket. He said as he slipped into the jacket, "Kane has a complaint to make, Miss Morrison. You might as well hear it, in the absence of your brother."

Pamela looked at Emmett, and Emmett said briefly, "A good part of your herd was driven into Vermilion Valley during that storm last night. Miss Wilson wants them out."

"In a blizzard," Boyd Halloran put in, "stock drifts with the wind. The valley was the nearest shelter."

"Crown stock was driven in last night," Emmett said flatly. "Our boys heard shots."

Pamela Morrison looked from Emmett to Halloran and then back again. She said to Halloran, "It should be an easy enough matter to run the stock out again, if they're on Miss Wilson's range."

"Easy enough," Halloran agreed, "but Kane put a time limit on it."

"If I didn't," Emmett observed, "you wouldn't bother until the spring."

"I'm sure," Pamela laughed, "we can settle this amicably."

"I'll wait until your brother gets back," Halloran said, "before I make any move."

Emmett looked at him steadily. "You drove that stock in without asking him about it," he said. "Why ask him if you can take them out?"

"Winter drift," Halloran smiled, "is never driven, except by snow and wind."

Pamela Morrison touched Emmett's arm before he could make any reply. She said, "Will you step up to the house a moment, Mr. Kane? We'll discuss the matter further."

Boyd Halloran was smiling blandly as Emmett followed the English girl up the lane and onto the porch of the main house. Curly Evans and the two Pine Tree riders moved back to their horses and waited for Emmett, watching the Crown men carefully.

Halloran went on into the barn, a satisfied expression on his face, as if he'd won his point.

On the porch Pamela turned and said slowly, "I suppose you have your orders from Miss

Wilson, and there's not much you can do about it."

Emmett nodded. "She wants the stock out of the valley. I told her I'd get them out. When is your brother due back?"

Pamela frowned. "All trains are held up, of course, due to the storm. He might not be able to get back before the end of the week."

"We can wait," Emmett told her. "If it was my valley I'd have made a deal with your brother a long time ago."

"Why won't Miss Wilson make a deal?"

Emmett shrugged. "Reckon she wants to keep the valley for herself. She's afraid if someone gets in she'll never get them out."

"My brother is not like that."

"Miss Wilson doesn't trust many people."

Pamela frowned. "Then she can't be happy," she said.

"She's not happy," Emmett agreed. "There's too much of her father in her. But she's a real woman."

"A very pretty one," Pamela said, and grinned. "Or haven't you noticed?"

"I've noticed," Emmett scowled.

Deftly, she changed the subject. She said, "Is it necessary for you to fight Halloran?"

"Out this way," Emmett told her, "you sometimes settle things differently. Halloran's been building up for a fight for a long time."

"You'll fight him again, then?"

Emmett nodded. He didn't tell her that the next time it could be with guns, and for good.

"I don't like it," she frowned. "You may be hurt."

She stopped, then, coloring slightly, and she looked away.

"I'm obliged," Emmett Kane murmured. This girl was interested in him, worried about him, and he didn't remember ever having met a woman before who'd been worried about him. Madge Wilson had never worried!

CHAPTER 14

Madge Wilson was waiting for them when they came back from the Crown ranch late that afternoon. She stood in the doorway as they dismounted out in front of the barn, and although she didn't say anything Emmett knew he was to report to her.

After he'd stabled the bay horse he'd been riding, he entered the house and found Madge sitting impatiently on the edge of a chair, her arms folded. He wondered if she was glad to see him back alive. His mission to Crown had been a dangerous one, and she knew it.

"How did you make out?" she asked abruptly.

Emmett sat down in a chair across from her, putting his hat on his knee.

"I promised Miss Morrison I'd wait till her brother got back from Cheyenne."

Madge's blue eyes snapped. "You promised Miss Morrison? Is she running Crown? What about Halloran?"

Emmett looked at her coldly. He said, "Halloran claims the stock in the valley is winter drift. He didn't want to touch them till the spring."

"And you believed him? He bluffed you, Emmett."

Emmett's gray eyes were hard. "I gave him

twenty-four hours to get his stuff out of the valley. Miss Morrison asked me to wait till her brother got back. There might not be any trouble that way."

"You had no right making a deal with her," Madge snapped.

Emmett didn't say anything for a moment. He sat with his hat in his hand. Finally he said, "You asked me to run this outfit, Miss Wilson. You want the job back?"

"I'm not asking you to quit," Madge said sullenly, "but you should have consulted me."

"You want us to run that stock out of the valley ourselves?" Emmett countered, "into Halloran's guns? If we wait a week, Morrison will get them out himself."

"How do we know he will?"

Emmett shrugged. "If he doesn't we'll take other steps. The week won't hurt anybody."

"I still don't like it," Madge told him tersely.

"You want us to fight Crown?" Emmett asked her. "There are four of us. Halloran has fifteen or twenty riders."

Madge didn't say anything to that, but she was still bitter. She said, "You made a bluff, and then the girl had you back down."

"She was talking sense," Emmett said, his anger rising. "She's only trying to avoid trouble."

"I want to avoid trouble, also," Madge observed, "but I have two thousand Crown stock in my valley."

Emmett stood up, his mouth tight. He said, "I can take a rifle now and shoot down every Crown beef I find in the valley. You think that will help? Halloran will come in here with his crew and burn you out. Then you'll have a range war on your hands."

"All right," Madge sulked. "We'll forget about it. We'll wait the week. But how do we know Morrison won't side with Halloran when he comes back?"

"I don't think he will," Emmett told her. "This was Halloran's deal from the beginning." He was thinking as he said this that one of Halloran's mistakes was that he didn't know how Clyde Morrison felt toward Madge Wilson. She was more than a neighbor.

As he was leaving he wondered, also, how Madge Wilson was going to take it when she learned that Dean Brockton had sold out to the Pine Tree foreman, and was pulling out. He'd have to tell her about that after Brockton left.

Back in the bunkhouse, Curly Evans said to him, "Reckon she didn't take it nice, Emmett."

Emmett shook his head.

"Some woman," Curly murmured, "like to see a fight. Others don't."

Dean Howlett said, "No lead coming at her, Curly."

"That ain't the way to figure it," Curly grinned. "In her way she's tougher than you, Dave."

"Ain't doubting that," Dave agreed.

"We don't do anything," Emmett said, "till Mr. Morrison gets back from Cheyenne. We'll let him give Halloran the orders."

Curly Evans said, "What do you figure Halloran's after, Emmett?"

"Everything he can get," Emmett told him. "He doesn't know he's already lost some of his best cards."

"How's that?" Curly asked curiously.

"He'll find out in a day or two."

Halloran found out the next morning. Old Ben Keefe, Brockton's lone hand, galloped up to Pine Tree a little before noon, chewing on his tobacco vigorously. When Curly Evans stepped out, Keefe yelled for Emmett Kane.

"What in hell's all the excitement about, Ben?" Curly grinned. "Looks like you're fixing to bust."

"Where's Kane?" Ben boomed.

Emmett had seen the old man coming in as he stood just inside the barn door. When he stepped out into the sunlight, Ben Keefe saw him and hobbled toward the barn as fast as he could walk.

"Old man's crazy," Curly chuckled.

Ben glanced back over his shoulder as he came up to Emmett, to make sure no one was coming behind him. He said in low tones, "Reckon you got to come back with me, boy."

"What happened?" Emmett asked.

"Ain't happened, yet," Ben scowled, "but

young Brockton's scared to hell, and asked me to ride over and get you. I was in the barn with him when Halloran and two of his boys rode up. He didn't even talk to Halloran. Just told me to get to hell over here, and not let Halloran see me going."

Emmett stepped back into the barn, slipped his saddle off a peg, and threw it across the roan. As he was working with the straps he said, "Anybody see you come?"

"I kept the barn between myself and Halloran's boys," Ben Keefe said proudly, "and I walked my horse away. I don't figure they saw me leave."

Emmett climbed into the saddle. "So Brockton's worried," he murmured.

"Scared as hell." Ben scowled. "Looked like he seen a ghost when Halloran come in sight."

"Thought he'd be on the train last night," Emmett said.

"No train going out. Maybe not till tonight. Had his bags packed, though. He ain't told me where he was going."

Emmett pushed the roan forward. "Better stay back here out of the way, Ben," he advised. "Might be trouble over at Bar B."

"Trouble's my middle name," Ben Keefe boasted. "Never run from it in my life, boy."

Curly Evans hurried down from the bunkhouse as Emmett rode past the corral. He yelled something, but Emmett motioned for him to remain at the ranch, and again he saw the disappointment in the little man's face.

Heading toward Squaw Run, he knew why Brockton was frightened. He'd undoubtedly made promises to Halloran, and Halloran was riding up now to make him carry out those promises. If he stalled, Halloran learned that he'd already sold Bar B, Dean Brockton would be a dead man.

The snow had started to melt again in the day's warm sunshine, and the roan splashed through the soft drifts and through the mud along the bank of Squaw Run. As he was breaking through the thin ice crossing the stream, he glanced back and saw Ben Keefe coming behind him.

It was less than two miles from Pine Tree to Bar B, and Emmett covered the distance in very good time. Riding up past the Bar B corral, he saw the two Crown hands squatting in the sunshine just outside the barn doorway, smoking. Halloran's chestnut horse was tied to the corral, but Halloran was nowhere in sight.

The Crown riders stood up, watching suspiciously as Emmett dismounted and walked toward the house. Ignoring them, he went up on the porch and rapped sharply on the door.

Dean Brockton had heard him coming, and the door opened immediately. Brockton's handsome face was white, and relief showed in his brown eyes. He said in a strained voice, "Come on in."

"Who's that?" Boyd Halloran said from inside the room.

Emmett pushed in through the door. Halloran was sitting in a chair by the open fireplace. His black, flat-crowned hat and checked jacket lay on the table nearby.

When Emmett came in, Halloran stood up, looking at Brockton suspiciously.

"What is this?" he asked slowly.

"You know Emmett Kane," Brockton mumbled.

"You know damn well that I know him."

Brockton sat down on the edge of a chair. He looked at Emmett, and then took a deep breath, and Emmett could see he'd been pinned against the wall here.

"All right," Brockton murmured. To Emmett he said, "Halloran has just offered to buy Bar B. He wants me to ride into Elkhorn with him this afternoon."

The statement hit Halloran like a blow in the face. He stared at Brockton as if the man were out of his mind, and for a moment he had nothing to say.

Emmett said it for him. "It's a good buy, Halloran, but you're too late."

Brockton got up from the chair, then, very nervous now, and he edged over in Emmett's direction, almost afraid to look at Halloran.

Halloran's voice was brittle, tense with emotion. "I'm too late?" he said slowly.

Emmett nodded. "I bought Bar B from Brockton two days ago."

For a long moment Halloran didn't say anything. He stared at Brockton, his turquoise eyes seeming to change color, and then he said softly, "You son of a bitch!"

"That won't do you any good," Emmett told him.

"You figured on pulling out before I knew anything about it," Halloran went on, still looking at Brockton.

"It was a business deal," Brockton muttered. "I have a right to sell my property any way I wish."

"We had an agreement," Halloran snapped.

"You forced me into it," Brockton said belligerently.

"Let's have no trouble," Emmett said, and smiled, "on my property. If you're finished, Halloran, you can ride out."

"I'll ride out," Halloran almost choked, "but I'm not through with you—either of you."

"You're through here," Emmett told him.

"You'll see more of me," Halloran promised. He picked up his jacket, put on his hat, and went out.

As the door closed behind him, Emmett realized that now it was war. Before they'd been sparring, but now Halloran intended to bring it out into the open. He'd been hit in a vital spot. Bar B had been the key to his success, and he'd lost the key.

Dean Brockton said dully, "He'll never let me get out of town now."

"There's a train leaving tonight?" Emmett said.

Brockton nodded. "If it had left last night," he muttered, "I'd have been gone." He looked at Emmett steadily, and then he said, "If you ride away from here, Kane, I'm a dead man."

"I'm not riding away," Emmett told him, and he saw the relief come into the man's eyes.

"You figure he'll come back with his crew?"

Emmett shrugged. "You'd be safer in town," he pointed out. "You have everything packed you want to take along?"

"I'm ready to go," Brockton told him.

Emmett stepped to the window and looked out. He saw Halloran and the two Crown hands riding away. Ben Keefe was watching them from the corral.

"Saddle up," Emmett ordered. "We'll ride into Elkhorn and ask Sheriff Freeman for protection. If Halloran tries anything then, he's running against the law—such as it is."

Brockton took a deep breath. "I'll get my bags," he said.

Emmett rolled a cigarette as he stepped out on the porch. Old Ben Keefe waddled toward him, stopping at the bottom step of the porch. He looked at Emmett carefully, and then he said, "Hell of a lot going on around here I don't know."

Emmett smiled at him as he drew on the cigarette after touching a match to it. He said, "You like it here, Ben?"

"It's okay," Ben nodded. "Considering all things."

"You can stay, then," Emmett told him. "I'll need a man who knows his way around."

Ben Keefe gaped. "I can stay?" he repeated.

"I own Bar B," Emmett said. "I'll need you around, Ben. Same deal you had with Brockton."

Ben Keefe exclaimed, "What about Brockton?"

"Going East," Emmett told him.

Ben rubbed his chin. "Where he belongs," he said softly. "He ain't like his father, and that's too damned bad. What about Miss Wilson?"

Emmett shrugged. "That's Brockton's business," he said. He was wondering, too, how Madge Wilson was going to accept her new neighbor, and how he would explain the fact that he'd gone about buying Bar B so secretly.

Brockton came out on the porch, carrying several suitcases. He said to the old man, "Think we can get a buckboard through to Elkhorn, Ben?"

Ben shook his head. "Doubt it. Better use a pack horse for that stuff."

"I'm leaving," Dean told him. "I've sold out, Ben."

"Just heard it," Ben said dryly. "Luck, boy."

Emmett didn't say anything. He watched the old man go out to the barn, and he smoked his cigarette. He said to Brockton eventually, "You have a message for Miss Wilson?"

Dean frowned. "Just tell her I felt that I had to go. She knows I've never been keen on ranching."

Emmett looked at the cigarette. "Nothing else?"

Dean Brockton bit his lips. "We never were engaged, or anything like that," he said rather crisply. "Just because we were brought up together people imagined things."

"I didn't say anything," Emmett told him.

Dean Brockton bit his lips. "Tell her I'm sorry," he said. "It's better this way."

Ben Keefe came out with a saddle horse and a pack horse. He tied the suitcases to the pack horse, and Dean Brockton climbed into the saddle.

"You're keeping Ben?" Brockton said to Emmett.

Emmett nodded.

"Ben's a good man," Dean said.

"Luck," Ben said again, and they rode off, following the vague outlines of the trace which led back to the stage road, and then into Elkhorn.

Dean Brockton rode on ahead with the pack horse, and Emmett followed. They rode in silence, the horses' hoofs clumping in the snow, and it was past noon when they entered Elkhorn's churned main street. The snow here had been trampled and rolled, melted and frozen by turn, and with the sun warm in the sky it was now a muddy slush through which the horses trampled, splashing the mud in all directions.

"Get your train ticket first?" Emmett asked.

Brockton nodded, and they rode down to the railroad station. The train was on the siding, ready to leave, and the station agent informed them that they expected to have the tracks cleared before nightfall, and that the eastbound would pull out at six.

"Five hours," Emmett said. "We'll eat."

They left the bags at the station and rode back into town, and Emmett could see the nervousness rising in Brockton.

"They won't shoot you off your horse in broad daylight," Emmett told him dryly.

"There's Hamp Freeman," Brockton said suddenly, and he rode over toward the Gunsight Saloon out of which Freeman had come.

Emmett followed him, smiling wryly. He sat his horse by the tie-rail in front of the saloon, watching Brockton talking rapidly to the sheriff. Freeman was bundled in a long black coat with a fur collar, and as Brockton spoke he kept looking at Emmett and frowning. Emmett couldn't hear what Brockton was saying, but it was evident Hamp Freeman wasn't too pleased with the whole business.

After a while Emmett dismounted, leading the roan up the alley of the Emerald Livery. He wasn't surprised to see Brockton hurrying after him, leading his own horse and the pack animal.

183

"What did Freeman say?" he asked over his shoulder.

"He thinks I'm imagining things," Brockton scowled. "He tells me I'm foolish to think Halloran will try to get back at me just because he lost a business deal."

"He say he'd stop Halloran if Halloran rode in here looking for you?"

"He said he'd preserve the peace in this town."

Emmett grinned. "We'll see," he said.

They stabled the horses, and then walked back to the lunchroom on the main street.

Sheriff Freeman was waiting for them on the corner, a cigar in his mouth, and his hands jammed into the pockets of his overcoat. He said to Emmett, "Sounds like a lot of damned foolishness to me."

"Does it?" Emmett smiled. "You should be wearing Brockton's coat."

Freeman looked at him curiously. "So you bought yourself a ranch," he murmured. "Doing pretty well for yourself in a short time, Kane."

"Held up a train last week," Emmett said. "Can I buy you a cup of coffee, Sheriff?"

Hamp Freeman looked at him silently, his round, puffy face grim, his weak chin thrust out, and then he walked away.

Emmett went into the lunchroom with Brockton and they sat at the counter, Brockton half facing the door. He wore a gun, and Emmett wondered vaguely if he'd have the nerve to use it if it came to a showdown with Halloran and his crew.

The girl brought them platters of bacon and eggs and they ate silently, both men lost in their own thoughts.

As he was sipping his coffee, Emmett said, "We'll get a room over at the hotel for the rest of the afternoon."

"You think that's best?" Brockton asked.

"You have any other ideas?" Emmett asked him.

"All right," Brockton said. "All right."

Emmett sat looking down at his coffee cup, wondering for the moment why he was doing this, risking being cut down by bullets from Crown riders. He had no particular use for Dean Brockton, and Brockton had permitted himself to get into this predicament because he'd been greedy for that extra money. The cards had fallen out the wrong way, and it was Brockton's deal to get himself out. But he'd said he'd stay, and he couldn't back down now.

He wondered if Halloran really would make an attempt to stop Brockton, knowing that Dean couldn't leave except by train. With almost a foot of snow on the ground, and more in the air, a man didn't move very far on horseback. The chances were that Halloran had a man in town already, keeping an eye on them.

When they finished eating, Brockton said, "It's two o'clock now."

"You could get a few hours' sleep before the train pulls out," Brockton told him.

Brockton just looked at him. "Sleep!" he muttered.

At the Cattleman's Hotel, Brockton signed up for a room. They were standing at the desk when Emmett saw Ben Keefe gallop up the street, his head moving from side to side as if looking for someone. He walked to the door rapidly.

The old man had dismounted out in front of the Gunsight Saloon, and Emmett whistled sharply, attracting his attention. Ben Keefe turned, and seeing Emmett on the hotel porch, walked that way.

Brockton came out and joined Emmett. He didn't say anything, but Emmett could hear him breathing heavily. Both men knew it wasn't good news Ben Keefe was bringing them.

"Halloran's riding in," Brockton muttered.

Ben Keefe came up on the hotel porch, puffing. He said to Emmett, "You the fellow just bought Bar B?"

"You know I am," Emmett said.

"Ain't much of it left by now," Ben told him, "except the land and what stock you got in the valley. You been burned out, boy."

Emmett looked at him. "Halloran?" he asked slowly.

"Dozen of 'em rode up," Ben Keefe explained. "Had bandanas over their faces, and they chased me to hell up in the hills. Whole place is burning down—barn and all."

"You see Halloran?" Emmett repeated.

"Couldn't recognize any of 'em," Ben said, "and they didn't give me much time to look. Couple of 'em opened up with Winchesters as they come down the grade to the corral. They were shooting too close for comfort. Halloran may have been there, but maybe not."

"That means they'll be coming here next," Brockton said dully.

Emmett didn't say anything. He went back into the hotel lobby, Ben following him, and bought a cigar at the desk. Biting off the tip, he stuck it in his mouth, and then he walked over to a chair by the window and sat down. He didn't light the cigar. He was thinking of the months he'd spent driving that trailherd up from Texas. Part of that money Boyd Halloran had just ruthlessly burned up.

Dean Brockton came over and said, "Tough, Kane. Wish I could do something."

Emmett waved a hand. "Forget it. I knew what I was getting into." To Ben Keefe he said, "Stick around, Ben. You see any Crown riders coming in, let me know."

"I'll watch fer 'em," Ben nodded, and he went outside after buying a cigar.

The lobby was empty save for the clerk behind the desk. Brockton took another chair which looked out on a window. He sat down heavily, and Emmett could see that there was little color in his face.

"It'll be a long afternoon," Brockton said.

Emmett didn't say anything to that. It would be a long afternoon, and an even longer night—if Boyd Halloran and the Crown crew were coming after him.

CHAPTER 15

At three in the afternoon Ben Keefe stepped into the lobby and said, "Two Crown boys just come in. Pulled up at the Wyoming Saloon."

Emmett nodded.

"Halloran ain't with 'em," Ben added.

"He'll come," Dean Brockton muttered.

Emmett got up and walked to the door. It had turned colder during the afternoon, and a few flakes of snow were sifting down out of a leaden sky. He said to Ben Keefe, "It ever stop snowing up this way?"

"Winter ain't even come, yet," Ben grinned. "Wait'll after Christmas. She really gets rough."

Emmett looked at the two Crown horses at the tie-rail out in front of the Wyoming Saloon, a short distance up the street. As he watched, one of the riders came out of the saloon to lead the animals up an alley into one of the barns back there. It meant that the Crown riders were staying around for a while.

As they watched, another pair of riders ambled down the main street where the slush was freezing. Emmett read the brand on the hips of the horses as they went by, both men turning in at the Okay Livery.

"Four of 'em," Keefe said.

"There'll be more," Emmett observed.

Dean Brockton got up and started to walk around the lobby. He said savagely, "I'm not sitting here and waiting for them to come in and shoot me down."

Emmett looked at him. "Either that, or you go out and shoot *them* down."

"Three more," Ben Keefe added, and Emmett looked through the window to watch three other Crown riders coming in from the west end of town, snow beginning to whiten the crowns of their hats.

The snow powdered the dirty, half-frozen slush, making it clean again. The wind rattled signs along the main street. It picked up an empty barrel out in front of a store across from the hotel, and rolled it down along the board walk. A black cat slinking out of an alley saw the barrel hurtling toward it, and went up an awning upright to sit on the roof and look down curiously.

Another Crown rider moved in on a dapple gray horse, head bent against the flying snow. He, too, went up the Okay Livery alley. Hamp Freeman came out of his office to talk for a few moments with Mark Randall, the lawyer, out in front of Randall's office, and then both men moved in opposite directions, Freeman walking under a wooden awning, the smoke from his cigar trailing behind him.

At four o'clock Curly Evans rode in, moving slowly down the street, evidently looking for someone. Emmett said to Ben Keefe, "Call him in, Ben. He wants to tell us about the fire."

Ben Keefe stepped out to the porch and signaled for Curly to come over. The Pine Tree rider dismounted and stepped into the lobby. He stared at Emmett and Brockton in surprise at finding them together, and then he said to Brockton, "Reckon you don't have a ranch house any more, Brockton."

Brockton just nodded at Emmett, and Emmett said, "I bought Bar B two days ago, Curly. My loss."

Curly's blue eyes widened. He tried to think of something to say, gave it up, and just shook his head.

"Miss Wilson know about it?" Emmett asked him.

Curly nodded. "We saw smoke an' rode over," he explained. "Miss Wilson went with us. What in hell happened?"

Emmett shrugged. "Ben Keefe figured Halloran's crew did it," he said.

Curly whistled softly. "Miss Wilson sent me in to look for Brockton. We didn't see him around the place."

"You see anyone?" Emmett asked.

Curly shook his head. "You sure it was Halloran?" he asked.

Emmett nodded.

Curly Evans shook the snow from his hat. "You

ain't riding for Pine Tree anymore," he said, disappointment in his voice.

"I'm a neighbor," Emmett told him. "Anybody hits at Pine Tree has to cross Bar B to do it."

Curly nodded, but Emmett could see he still didn't like the setup. Curly Evans didn't like to ride for a woman boss.

"Miss Wilson know about this?" Curly asked.

"Not yet," Emmett said. "She'll find out."

Curly glanced at Dean Brockton, who'd sat down in the chair again, and it was evident that he had many more questions to ask but realized he had no right to ask them. He said, "You expectin' trouble, Emmett?"

"I'll find out."

"When you find out," Ben Keefe put in, "you might be dead."

"I'll stick around," Curly murmured. "Ain't doing nothin' this afternoon, anyway."

"Bar B's fight," Emmett said. "You're not in it, Curly."

Curly shrugged. "Can't anybody chase me out of town," he observed. "I'll be over in the Longhorn if anybody asks for me."

He went out through the door and they watched him cross the road, leading his horse, and then taking the horse up an alley to a rear stable.

Ben Keefe said grimly, "Town's crowding up, Kane, but the big guy ain't here yet."

"He'll come," Emmett said. . . .

At five o'clock it was already dark. The wind was blowing, rattling the signs, whistling down the street.

Old Ben Keefe, who'd been in and out of the lobby all afternoon, came in slapping his gloved hands together.

"Damn snow keeps up there might not be a train leaving tonight," he commented.

Brockton got up, breathing heavily. "There has to be a train," he snapped.

Emmett looked at him. "We could step out for a bite to eat," he said. "Be time to board the train by then."

"I'd rather wait here," Brockton answered.

Emmett noticed that he stayed away from the windows now, but still nothing had happened. Ben Keefe had spotted other Crown riders drifting into town, but none of them had come toward the hotel, or made any attempt to look for them.

The minutes moved by slowly. At half-past five Dean Brockton said thickly, "They'll be waiting for us when we step out of here."

"Wouldn't hurt," Emmett advised, "to get down to the station now and board the train."

Brockton looked at him. "All right," he nodded.

"Take a look around, Ben," Emmett ordered.

Ben stepped out on the porch, and poked his head back inside.

"All clear," he said.

Emmett left his jacket open so that he could

reach the gun easily. He said, "Ready, Brockton?"

Dean Brockton took a deep breath. He nodded, not trusting his voice. His face was the color of ashes, and his eyes were dead.

Emmett stepped out onto the porch, and Brockton followed him, closing the door immediately. They went down the porch steps, and Emmett called back over his shoulder, "Stay there, Ben."

"Hadn't figured on going along," Ben said dryly.

It was full dark now. The main street of Elkhorn was deserted. There were no horses at the tie-racks, every rider coming into town have stabled his horse. It was one long block to the railroad station at the south end of town. They could see the train at the station, the light from its windows falling across the snow.

They started down the walk side by side, and as they approached the first alley, Emmett took his gun from the holster and held it in his hand. He heard Brockton do the same thing.

A man came out of the Wyoming Saloon, stopped to light a cigarette, and they slowed down, but the man crossed the road before they came up to him, not even looking in their direction, and entered a house on the opposite side of the street.

They passed two alleys, swinging out wide as they approached each one, but both were empty. They were within fifty yards of the train, and then twenty-five, and Emmett could hear Brockton breathing hard.

A number of other passengers were getting aboard the train as they came up. Mail and baggage was going into the baggage car.

"They might have somebody on board," Brockton said.

Emmett nodded. "We'll have a look through each car before the train pulls out," he said.

They were at the station now, walking along beside the four passenger cars. There were few passengers getting aboard. This was the railhead for the line, and the train had been idle on the siding all day. It was empty as it prepared to move east.

They got aboard, Emmett going first. Then they walked the length of the four cars, forward and then back, Emmett taking the lead as they went up the aisles.

There were about fifteen people aboard, a few women, a child, several men who could have been drummers or businessmen returning to the East—and no one whom Brockton could identify as a Crown man.

It was still ten minutes before the train was due to leave, and Brockton was beginning to perk up as he took a seat in the second car from the last.

"Halloran must have changed his mind," he said to Emmett. "He burned you out and decided to let it go at that."

Emmett shook his head. The fact that Halloran had made no attempt on Brockton's life was mystifying. He'd been positive the Crown ram-rod wouldn't let Brockton slip away from Elkhorn that easily. There was the possibility someone would come up and put a bullet through the window just before the train pulled out. He said to Brockton, "Keep that gun handy until you're well out of Elkhorn. I'll wait outside until the train leaves."

Dean Brockton looked at him. "I'm obliged," he said. "You didn't have to do this, Kane."

Emmett shook his head. "Good luck," he said, and that was their parting. He wondered how Brockton felt about leaving Madge Wilson this way. All afternoon he'd said nothing about Madge, his mind on his own survival. He had no word for Madge now.

Out on the platform, Emmett stepped back into the shadows. He watched both ends of the string of cars. Smoke was gushing up from the smokestacks, and the engine was throbbing. No more passengers got aboard. Emmett kept his hand on his gun, and stood back in the snow out of the light of the cars.

The conductor was talking to the station agent out in front of the waiting-room at the far end of the station, and then the conductor stepped aboard after flashing a lantern to the engineer.

Dean Brockton sat away from the window, and Emmett could see him indistinctly through the fogged glass. The train started to roll forward.

Brockton disappeared, and Emmett started to relax, wondering if this long afternoon of vigilance had been unnecessary after all. Then as he glanced down toward the waiting-room he saw a shadow slide out from behind the building and step aboard the last car on the rear platform. He wondered how he could have been so foolish as to think Halloran would forget.

Moving out from the shadows, gun in hand, he waited as that last car drew near him. As it rolled by he lifted the gun, holding it steady. Behind him, from the direction of a ramshackle barn, he heard a man shout, and then the rear platform slid past and he caught a glimpse of a man crouched there. A thin crack of yellow light came through the doorway, falling across the man's face as he moved.

The man was Pete Cooley, and he had a gun ready in his hand. Cooley had heard that warning shout, too, and he was ready. His gun winked in the night, but Emmett was moving to his right as the train rolled left, and he made a poor target even at such close range.

Cooley's bullet tore into the wood of the platform to Emmett's right. Emmett fired twice, just as a gun opened up on him from the rear. Pete Cooley was smashed back against the door by the impact of the bullets, and then the forward movement of the train propelled him the other way, and he slumped over the iron railing, his hat falling from his head, both arms dangling, the gun dropping from his limp fingers. He was hanging that way, lifeless, when the train rolled into the night.

Emmett swung with his gun, threw two quick shots in the direction of the barn, and then started to run down toward the waiting-room. A fusillade of shots followed him, and then he heard Boyd Halloran's flat voice:

"Get him—get him!"

The long night had begun.

CHAPTER 16

The station master came out of his waiting-room to stare as Emmett sprinted past him, swinging around the building and heading up behind the row of houses on the east side of Elkhorn's main street. As he ran he broke the gun, clicked out the spent shells and shoved in fresh ones.

The snow was deep back here in the vacant lots, and it was hard running, but it was also very dark. He could hear shouting men coming after him, and once when he glanced back a gun flashed several times as one of his pursuers opened up on a shadow.

Emmett stumbled over a hillock, slid down the other side, and then plunged down an alley to the main street. He took one look up and down the street, and then crossed rapidly, turning up the alley of the Okay Livery.

The stable door at the far end of the alley was ajar, a crack of yellow lantern light showing on the snow. Inside, he found the stable empty. There were a few horses in the stalls, and he deliberated for a moment, wondering if he ought to take a horse here or attempt to get his own horse from the Emerald Livery. But he realized that would only postpone the issue. Boyd Halloran had fired the first gun, and the fight was joined. If it stopped

199

here it would start up again another day, and unless he ran away he would have to face it. Tonight was as good a time as any.

Ascending the ladder to the loft, Emmett dropped down on the hay, resting for a few minutes while he decided upon a course of action. There were at least a dozen Crown riders in town, and Halloran would have all of them out looking for him, scattering as they moved up the street. He hoped he would find Halloran alone, or with not too many of his crew at hand. They would be searching the alleys now, looking into the back rooms of saloons, in stables. Eventually they would be coming in here.

He heard the door squeak beneath him, and he slid the gun out of the holster, wondering if they'd found him. Someone came into the stable, pausing just inside the door. Back in the shadows, Emmett inched forward to look, and then he heard Curly Evans's soft whisper.

"Emmett?"

"All right," Emmett murmured.

Curly stepped over to the ladder. "Saw you come in here," he said. "Hell of a lot of shooting down at the station. They get Brockton?"

"He's all right," Emmett told him. "Halloran's after me now."

There was a pause below, and then Curly said, "You signing on a crew, Emmett?"

Emmett smiled. "After tonight," he said.

"Might be too late after tonight," Curly scowled. "You need hands now."

"You better stay with Pine Tree."

"Not me," Curly said grimly. "Reckon this wouldn't of happened if Miss Wilson had leased the valley to Morrison."

"Too late for that now," Emmett said.

"Tell her," Curly growled. "She's in town."

"Miss Wilson's in Elkhorn?"

"Rode in a few minutes ago," Curly explained. "Reckon she knows something's going on, and she doesn't know what. She had to come in to see. She's at the hotel."

Emmett thought that it was typical of Madge Wilson not to sit home and wait for the news to come to her. Emmett had been gone most of the day from Pine Tree, and Dean Brockton's place had burned down, with Brockton gone. She had to know what was happening. In this weather, the chances were she'd remain at the hotel overnight.

"What do you figure on doing?" Curly asked curiously.

"Stay away from them until the fight is more even."

"That might take a hell of a long time."

"I have time," Emmett said, and then he climbed down from the loft and stepped to the door, looking out carefully.

"Reckon I ought to be in this some way," Curly said stubbornly. "Ain't right, a dozen against one."

"They'll get in their own way tonight," Emmett smiled, "and it's a good night for hiding."

He slipped out through the door, leaving Curly in the barn. Instead of returning down the alley to the main street, he moved along the rear of the buildings, keeping well back in the shadows. The snow was coming down harder now; it was deep back here in the vacant lots. He moved without haste, watching the alleys as he came to them, and when he reached a building which appeared to be deserted, he stepped in through the rear door, which was open.

The building, as he remembered it, adjoined the Longhorn Saloon. The front had been a store, but the window was now boarded up. Feeling his way carefully, Emmett moved up to the front of the building and looked out through the cracks between the boards. He saw two men come out of the alley directly across the way and look up and down the street before crossing. Another man came down the alley from the Emerald Livery, joining these two, and they left footprints in the new snow as they crossed the street, disappearing from sight.

Emmett stepped back from the boarded window, his hands coming in contact with a chair nearby. He sat down, reached inside his jacket for his tobacco, and rolled a cigarette. He smoked it through, and then he got up and had another look out through the crack in the window.

It was then that he heard the door creak behind him, and when he turned he saw the darker shadow in the opening. Stepping back from the boarded window, he drew his gun soundlessly and waited. The man in the doorway had paused there, and then another man came up behind him. They both came inside, and Emmett was positive now that they'd seen his footprints outside.

He could no longer see them now because they'd stepped to either side of the doorway. When a third man appeared in the entrance he knew that it was time to go. He heard a boot scrape cautiously on the wooden floor, and lifting the sixgun he fired three times, aiming high, the sound filling the room. Then he kicked out two of the boards across the store window and dived through, just as guns opened up on him.

He rolled in the snow as he hit the walk, and then scrambling to his feet he sprinted north, running past the Longhorn Saloon. A man raced out of the alley of the Okay Livery across the way, and seeing him, dropped to one knee and opened fire.

Emmett pulled up next to an awning upright, steadied his gun against the post, and fired once. When the man across the road tumbled slowly forward into the snow he started to run again.

He was going past the hotel front when he heard Madge Wilson calling sharply, "Emmett— Emmett!"

She was on the porch in the shadows, and Emmett went up the steps in two quick leaps. Taking her arm he pushed her in through the doorway to the lobby, closing the door behind him. Down the street he could hear men shouting, and he knew he couldn't stay here long.

Madge said tersely, "Who is it, Emmett?"

"Halloran and his crew," Emmett told her. He pointed toward the stairs and said, "We have a room up there. I can't stay here."

Madge nodded and hurried toward the stairs. Emmett pointed a finger at the clerk as he went by, and cautioned, "You didn't see me tonight."

The man behind the desk nodded. Emmett hurried up the stairs behind Madge Wilson. She waited for him on the landing and he pointed to Room 11, the one Dean Brockton had registered for that afternoon.

They stepped inside, Emmett leaving the door open until he could find the lamp and touch a match to it. When he'd turned the lamp up he closed the door and stepped to the window, pulling the shade back slightly to look out.

He couldn't see the walk directly beneath because the porch roof extended out some distance from the building. He saw two men running south on the opposite side of the street, heading down toward the man who'd been shot. He didn't think they'd seen him enter the hotel lobby, which meant he was safe here for a time.

When he turned around he saw Madge watching him.

"I'd like to know what this is all about, Emmett," she said.

Emmett took off his hat and slapped the snow from it, and then he sat on the edge of a chair as he inserted fresh cartridges into the gun cylinder. He said, without looking at her, "Halloran's out to kill me because I bought Brockton's Bar B."

Madge said slowly, "You bought Bar B?"

Emmett nodded. "That's why Halloran burned me out this afternoon."

"Where is Dean?" Madge asked him.

"Went out on the eastbound night train."

"He left the country—for good?"

Emmett nodded. He didn't look at her. He said, "Halloran was trying to buy Bar B, so that he could cut you off from Squaw Creek and freeze you out of Vermilion Valley. His play was to get Clyde Morrison to sell out to him, and then with Crown, Bar B, and your valley he'd be head man in this part of the country."

"That the reason Halloran ran Crown stock into the valley without Morrison knowing about it?"

"That's the reason. He wanted to keep Morrison in hot water all the time, and he wanted you to fight back at Crown so that you'd never lease the valley to Morrison. If this turned out to be a tough winter, Morrison would have quit, and Halloran would step in."

Madge Wilson was silent for a moment, and then she said, "Where did Dean figure in here? Had he made a deal with Halloran?"

Emmett shrugged. "Brockton wanted to get out. I offered him good money for the outfit."

"More than Halloran had offered?"

Emmett looked at her. "How would I know if Halloran made an offer?"

"You're lying," Madge said flatly, and Emmett's mouth tightened. "Where did you get the money to buy a ranch?" she asked. "You were riding for me for fifty dollars a month."

Emmett stepped to the window again to look out around the shade. When he came back he said, "That trailherd I brought up from Texas belonged to me."

"And you were posing as a loose rider."

"You took me for that," Emmett told her tightly. "I never said I was broke."

"Why did you sign with me, then?"

"Had time on my hands," Emmett growled, "and I was curious. Had to find out something."

He'd found it out, too. This girl was not for him. He knew that very definitely now, and he also knew it had been worth buying Bar B to find out.

"What are you going to do with Bar B now that you have it?" Madge asked him.

Emmett looked at her. "Sell it to you," he said.

Madge frowned. "Why did you buy it?"

"I don't like Halloran," Emmett stated.

Down below he could hear men coming into the lobby.

Madge Wilson said woodenly, "You'll sell to me, then, and pull out the way Brockton did."

Emmett shrugged. He stepped to the lamp and turned it down until only a tiny flame showed. He said, "If I live."

Madge sat down on the edge of the bed. She looked at him, a dull expression on her face. She knew, too, that it was over between them.

Emmett said, just before blowing out the light, "You might make a deal with Morrison now. I think he'll be glad to have you as a neighbor."

He saw interest and speculation come into her eyes, and realized that she wasn't hurt permanently. He thought how right Morrison would be for her. Both were hard, but she would have respect for Clyde Morrison, something she never would have had for Dean Brockton.

As he stepped to the window in the darkened room, raised the shade, and lifted the window sash quietly, Madge Wilson said to him, "You might make a deal with Morrison's sister, Emmett. Think of that before you ride away from here."

Emmett thought about it as he stepped through the window to the porch roof, closing the window behind him. He crouched, and then moved cautiously along the roof until he came to the corner of the building. The Cattleman's Hotel occupied the entire corner, the porch roof running in both directions.

Emmett slipped around into the shadows, moved down to the opposite end of the porch, and then lowered himself from the roof and dropped into the snow beneath. As he landed with a soft thud he heard a man running across the wooden porch floor, and then a quick shout: "There he is!"

A gun roared from close up, and he felt the sting as the bullet grazed his left shoulder, tearing through his jacket. Squatting in the snow, he fired up through the porch railing, aiming hurriedly at the dark shape closing in on him. He heard the man's body hit the porch floor with a heavy thud, and then he turned and ran down the dark sidestreet. As he ran he felt the warm blood sliding down his arm and dripping from his fingers.

This narrow street ended in open country, and when Emmett reached the last shack on the street he swung west again, heading back in the direction of the railroad station.

He could hear men pounding after him in the snow, and once he stopped to send several shots back at them, making them scatter. He saw their guns wink in the falling snow, and then he plunged on through the drifts, trying to reload on the run. He could feel pain in that shoulder wound now, even though he knew it was not bad.

He kept running parallel to the main street, passing one alley after the other. As he neared the last row of buildings, two men plunged out of the alley, heading straight for him. They were less than ten yards away when they opened up on him with their guns. He'd been running at top speed, and just as the guns roared his left foot went down into a pothole concealed by the snow. As he lurched forward, off balance, something smashed him in the left shoulder. It was like a hammer blow, spinning him, deadening the arm and shoulder, and he went down, rolling.

When he came up on his knees he had the gun working, spitting flame. Another bullet flicked the brim of his hat, but he was a poor target now, down in the snow, and both Crown riders were standing up.

The first man doubled at the waist and pitched forward in the snow when Emmett's lead struck him. He landed on his right shoulder, rolled, and lay still.

The second man was knocked back by the impact of the bullet, and he staggered in the snow, like a drunken man, his hat falling from his head. He started to shoot, emptying his gun at the sky as he stumbled, dropped to his knees, and then fell on his back in a deep bank of snow.

Emmett, clutching his left shoulder, staggered over to look down at him, and then heard the shouts of the men behind him. He turned down the alley out of which the two Crown men had come.

He tried to reload the gun as he ran, but the fingers of his left hand were numb. He knew he wasn't going to leave this town of Elkhorn tonight.

As he stumbled out of the alley to the main street, a man darted out at him, and he raised the empty gun to slash at him crazily. He heard Curly Evans's voice.

"Emmett—Emmett. No!"

Curly caught him as he started to fall, and then another man came up on the other side of him, supporting him. He felt nauseous now, and there was no strength left in his body. He tried to tell Curly to let him alone or Halloran's crew would cut him down too, but Curly wasn't paying any attention to him.

He was helped into a stable, and the two men got him up on a horse, tying him there as securely as they could, and the horse was led out into the snow again.

Gradually, as they rode along in the darkness, the snow swirling around them, he became conscious of the fact that the second man was Ben Keefe, and old Ben was cursing steadily, grimly, as they rode along.

After a while Ben left them, and Curly Evans rode close beside him, supporting him in the saddle. Pain started to come, then, after the first shock of the wound had passed.

"Pretty bad?" Curly asked him once. "Ben's gone to get Doc Brown."

"Where are we going?" Emmett mumbled.

"Only damn place in these parts Halloran won't think to look," Curly chuckled. "Crown ranch."

Despite the pain, Emmett had to grin. Pamela Morrison would be at the ranch, and Ben Keefe was bringing the doctor out to take care of the bullet hole. In the morning, when he felt better, he would have another go at Boyd Halloran. He wished fervently, though, that Halloran had come in line with his gun this night.

He lost track of time as they rode along through the snow. He knew they weren't going very fast because Ben Keefe and Doc Brown caught up with them before they raised the lights of Crown ranch. The physician, a wizened little man with a sharp face, held a bottle to his lips.

The whiskey was warm in Emmett's throat and all through his body. He heard Brown say to Curly Evans, "Should have thought to bring some liquor along with you. You want the man to freeze to death?"

"Hell," Curly told him, "we didn't have time to stop for drinks, Doc. We were damn lucky to get out of town alive."

Doc Brown grumbled something, and Curly rode on ahead to make sure no Crown hands saw them coming in.

"Ain't likely there'll be any of 'em around," Curly said before he left, "but we can't take chances."

"Where's the law?" Doc Brown snapped.

"Ain't much law on a night like this," Curly chuckled.

He came back in a few minutes with the news that Pamela Morrison was alone at the ranch house, with only the Chinese cook out in the bunkhouse, and he was usually in bed at this hour. Pamela was preparing a room for Emmett.

They rode up to the door quietly, and Curly and Ben Keefe helped Emmett from the horse, half carrying him into the house. Pamela stood by the entrance, and Emmett had a look at her face as they helped him in. He saw the horror and the concern there, and he tried to smile at her.

"How bad is he?" Pamela asked. She pointed to a doorway and the two men helped Emmett in, sitting him on a bed in the room.

"Got a bullet through the shoulder," Curly explained, "and he lost plenty of blood. But he's tough."

"I want to help," Pamela said.

"Digging a bullet out of a man is not pleasant business, ma'am," Doc Brown told her. "We'll call you in when it's over."

Pamela looked down at Emmett, her dark eyes soft. She said quietly, "You're safe here, Mr. Kane."

CHAPTER 17

It was past midnight when Doc Brown left. Ben Keefe had ridden off with the horses, so that Halloran wouldn't find them when he returned. Emmett lay on the bed, the left shoulder bandaged securely. Curly Evans had his blanket in a corner of the room, having refused to leave.

"Ain't likely they'll come walking in here," Curly had stated, "but if they do they'll have another gun on 'em."

Emmett watched Pamela Morrison clearing away the few dishes from the table beside the bed. She'd made some broth for him, and coffee for Curly and the doctor. Emmett said to her, "We shouldn't have gotten you mixed up in this, Miss Morrison."

"It's our crew that's trying to do the killing," Pamela told him. "Mr. Halloran never comes into the house, and you will be safe here until Clyde returns. He may be on the train that's due in tomorrow."

"Snow's stopped," Curly said. "Wasn't too bad this time, and maybe the trains will be running." He stepped to the window to listen. "Riders coming in now," he grinned. "Had enough snow to hide our tracks when we come in here, so Halloran won't know nothing."

Emmett looked at the gun on the chair beside him. He saw the English girl look at it, too, and again that fear came into her eyes. When she'd gone out with the dishes, Curly Evans said softly, "There's a real girl, Emmett."

Emmett didn't say anything. He lay on the bed, looking up at the ceiling, feeling the throb in his shoulder.

"Reckon Halloran's mad enough to eat nails," Curly Evans was saying. "He didn't get Brockton as he thought he would, and he didn't get you, either. When Morrison returns to Elkhorn he's through here, him and his crew."

"He won't ride away," Emmett stated, "until he sees me."

"You ain't seeing him till you get out of that bed," Curly said. "I'll take care of that."

"I'll be up in the morning," Emmett murmured.

"But you won't be standing up to a man with a gun," Curly scowled. "He'll cut you down, Emmett."

"He'll try to," Emmett said.

Curly was still scowling as he came over to blow out the lamp. He had another look out through the window before he curled up on the floor in his blanket. Emmett heard him mumbling to himself before he dropped off to sleep. . . .

When Emmett awoke in the morning, bright sunlight streaming in through the room, he noticed that Curly was gone. He was putting on his boots,

214

and having difficulty doing it, when Curly came in with his breakfast, Pamela Morrison following him.

"Wouldn't hurt none," Curly said disapprovingly, "to spend another day in bed. Doc Brown said it'd do you good."

"I'll stiffen up in bed," Emmett told him. "Better to move around a little."

"Halloran rode off with most of his crew this morning," Pamela told him. "There are a few men around, but they won't come near the house."

"He rode off?" Emmett murmured.

"Reckon he's headed for Pine Tree," Curly said, "to see if you're holing up there. He knows by now you got out of Elkhorn."

Emmett looked at the breakfast they'd brought in for him. He nodded his appreciation to Pamela and she smiled at him.

"When you've finished," she said, "I'm going to dress that wound. Doctor Brown told me how."

"This afternoon," Emmett said, "if Halloran isn't around, I'll ride out."

Curly stared at him, and Pamela said hastily, "But you can't! You have no place to go, and you have a bullet wound."

Emmett shook his head. "If Halloran finds me here there'll be gunplay, even if your brother is around. I don't want that."

"Where in hell will you go?" Curly argued. "Halloran burned you out yesterday."

"I'll hole up in one of Bar B line shacks," Emmett told him. "If Halloran looks for me then he'll find me."

"When he finds you," Curly growled, "you'll be dead."

Emmett shrugged as he sipped his coffee. "Ben Keefe and I can hide out until this shoulder heals."

"My brother will have the whole thing straightened out by then. Halloran won't be with us anymore," Pamela urged.

Emmett shook his head. "They had to bring me here last night," he said. "It was the only place I could go where Halloran wouldn't think to look for me. Today, I can move. I'll take care of myself."

"Can't we notify Sheriff Freeman?" Pamela asked.

Curly Evans laughed briefly. "Hamp is always in the wrong place when the shooting starts," he said. "Reckon he doesn't have too much use for Emmett anyway."

"Then there's nothing anyone can do," Pamela said hopelessly. She watched Emmett, who was eating calmly.

Looking up at her, Emmett said, "I don't aim to die, ma'am."

When he'd finished breakfast he got up and walked around the room a few times, getting the feel of his legs. His left arm was bandaged to his side, but his right arm was free. The shoulder still throbbed, and it was stiff, but he'd had a good night's sleep, and breakfast had given him back his strength. He said to Pamela, "How many Crown hands are still here?"

"Two," she said.

Emmett strapped on his gunbelt, Curly Evans helping him. "Can you send them in to town on an errand," he asked, "and then let us have two of your horses? We'd be better to move out now while Halloran is still gone."

Pamela looked at Curly Evans, and Curly shook his head as if to say that there was nothing he could do.

"All right," she nodded.

From the window Emmett watched as she went out to the barn and spoke to the two men there. After a while they saddled up and headed in toward Elkhorn.

Pamela came back and said, "There are plenty of horses."

Far in the distance they could hear a train whistle, and Curly Evans said, "Reckon that's the westbound coming in from Cheyenne. Your brother will be on that, Miss Morrison."

The English girl looked at Emmett quickly. "Clyde will be here in an hour or so now. Won't you wait?"

"Better for all of us," Emmett told her, "if I get away from here."

Curly Evans shook his head and went out

to saddle two horses. Emmett, wearing one of Clyde Morrison's shirts, automatically reached up to the pocket for his tobacco pouch. He saw it on the dresser, and stepped over that way to pick it up.

Pamela smiled a little and took the pouch from him. "I'll roll your cigarette," she said. "I've been watching Clyde do it." Emmett nodded and sat down on the edge of a chair to watch her.

She said as she worked with the tobacco and cigarette paper, "I understand you've bought Bar B."

"Selling it back to Miss Wilson," Emmett told her. "Halloran was trying to buy it in order to squeeze Pine Tree out of Vermilion Valley."

Pamela looked up at him curiously. "You were protecting Miss Wilson, then."

Emmett shrugged. "I had the money," he stated, "and I wouldn't lose anything on it."

"Except your life," Pamela observed. She looked down at the cigarette in her fingers, and said, "Madge Wilson seems to be a nice girl."

"A stubborn one," Emmett told her, "and with too much pride for a woman. If she'd leased Vermilion Valley to your brother in the beginning she'd have stopped Halloran then."

Pamela seemed to brighten a little. "Clyde likes proud women," she laughed. "He's told me that before." She came over and handed him the cigarette. "What kind do you like?"

Emmett stood up and looked down at her, the cigarette in his hand. He said, "You've been worried about me."

"Yes," she said.

He acted very simply, and very gently. Putting his right arm around her, he drew her close, and she looked up at him, smiling a little, her dark eyes shining. When he kissed her she put her arms around his neck. She was still smiling when he released her.

"I'd like you to see Texas, Pamela," he said.

"I've wanted to see it," Pamela told him.

"I'll come back when Halloran's gone."

"I'll be waiting for you."

He went out and found Curly Evans waiting with the two horses. Pamela came out on the porch to watch them. She stood there, oblivious to the cold, as Emmett hoisted himself into the saddle. He touched his hat to her, and she lifted a hand as he rode off.

Curly said as they crossed a field of snow, "I'm picking up Dave and Ben, and bringing 'em back to where you'll be."

"Not their fight," Emmett told him.

"They'll make it their fight," Curly growled. "There's a Bar B line shack up along the west spur of Squaw Run. I'll see you fixed up there, and then I'll have Ben Keefe take you some supplies. I'll be back with Dave and Ben, and maybe a few more, if I can get 'em."

"You'll make it a real war," Emmett observed. "It's only a little one now."

"Big enough to kill a man," Curly said.

They swung west from Crown ranch, and in half an hour hit Squaw Run, frozen over and covered with snow.

It was past noon when they reached the line shack. Curly got in some wood and started the fire. He fixed up the bunk with blankets, making it as comfortable as possible.

The ride had weakened Emmett, and he was glad to sit down on the edge of the bunk.

"Ben's over at Pine Tree," Curly said. "I told him to head over there last night. Send him right back here with a coffee pot and some grub."

"You might run into Halloran," Emmett told him.

Curly shrugged. "I'll try to steer clear of him," he said. "If he asks, I'll tell him you're headed fer Texas. He doesn't even know you've been hit."

"Tell Ben to bring extra blankets," Emmett said, "and a rifle."

"He'll be along in an hour," Curly told him. "Just sit tight."

When the Pine Tree rider had left, Emmett stepped to the door to look out before going back to the bunk. He placed the Colt on the floor within reach of his arm, and then he lay down and closed his eyes. . . .

It was midafternoon when he heard a lone horse

clumping through the snow toward the shack. Gun in hand, Emmett stepped to the door and looked out.

Ben Keefe was just dismounting, lifting a heavy saddlebag from the saddle. The old man looked at Emmett critically as he came out into the open, and said, "More life in you than there was last night."

Emmett held the door open for him. He looked down along Ben's backtrail, and Ben said, "Nobody followed me, Kane. Halloran pulled out before Curly come in to Pine Tree. Miss Wilson sent me right out here with grub and blankets. Curly's coming along later. Said something about seeing Mr. Morrison in town."

Emmett frowned. "What about Halloran?" he asked.

"Had ten men with him when they come up to Pine Tree," Ben Keefe explained. "Miss Wilson give him hell, and they rode off. Heard Halloran telling his crowd to head back to Crown. He was riding in to Elkhorn."

"Riding in alone?"

Ben Keefe looked at him, and at the bandaged arm. "Halloran rode off alone," he nodded.

Emmett sat down on the bunk. "Make me a pot of coffee, Ben," he said, "and then throw a saddle on that horse under the lean-to in back."

Ben Keefe squatted down in front of the fire, throwing a few more chunks of wood on it. He said over his shoulder, "Curly says you were holing up here for a while."

"Changed my mind," Emmett smiled.

"You figure you'll settle it now," Ben murmured, "in Elkhorn."

"You said he was alone."

"He rode in alone," Ben Keefe nodded. "He's got two arms, and you got one, Emmett."

"Only need one," Emmett smiled. "Make that coffee hot, Ben. . . ."

An hour later he rode away from the line shack, Ben Keefe staring after him from the doorway, shaking his head grimly. He rode with the left sleeve of his leather jacket flapping, the arm bound against his side inside the jacket.

He followed Squaw Run, seeing the smoke from Pine Tree ranch inside Vermilion Valley as he rode past the mouth of the valley, and then he hit into the old stage road, turning south toward Elkhorn. He saw no one as he rode along. He thought once of swinging south earlier and having a look at his burned ranch house, but he decided against it. Halloran might have a few of his crew in the vicinity, waiting for just such a move.

He passed some of his own stock down in the hollows, and made a mental note to have Ben Keefe run them into the valley. The stock would be Madge Wilson's in a few days anyway, after he'd made his deal with her. He wondered, though, if he would be alive after tonight to make any deals.

Then he thought of Pamela Morrison, and knew he had to live.

The sun dropped early these winter days, and the lights were twinkling on in Elkhorn when he came in sight of the town. As he came down the grade into town he wondered what Halloran's errand here had been. Possibly the Crown ramrod had gone into town to meet Clyde Morrison, giving him his distorted side of the affair of last evening. Halloran might still think he could swing the big deal he'd had in mind from the beginning, and he might this moment be trying to convince Morrison that he'd be better off to sell Crown.

Emmett rode down the grade into town, approaching it from the north. It was nearly dusk when he entered the snowy mud-churned main street, turning in at the first livery stable. His shoulder was aching badly again after the ride, and he realized that he'd have to finish this business as soon as possible.

The livery man took his horse.

"Halloran in town?" Emmett asked him.

The man looked at the empty sleeve. "Seen him down at the Longhorn earlier in the afternoon," he said. "You bust that arm?"

"Hurt it," Emmett nodded. He slipped his tobacco pouch from inside his shirt pocket and handed it to the man. "This is hard on a one-arm man," he said.

The stable man rolled the cigarette for him, and

Emmett put it into his mouth, touching a match to it. He sat down on a bale of hay just inside the stable door, smoking and looking down at the floor, and then he said, "Boyd Halloran a friend of yours?"

The stable man grinned. He said, "Halloran don't have too many friends in this town."

Emmett took a bill from his pocket and placed it on the bale of hay. He said, "Take that with you, and tell me where Halloran is now."

The man rubbed his chin thoughtfully. "Reckon that's easy money," he murmured. "You the fellow them Crown riders was after last night?"

Emmett didn't answer. He sat on the bale, smoking the cigarette, and then the stable man picked up the bill and went out.

The cigarette was almost smoked through when he came back. He said briefly, "Halloran's having his supper in Windy Conway's lunchroom."

"Alone?"

"He's alone."

Emmett pitched the cigarette butt out through the door. He got up and walked out into the alley, the stable man watching him go without saying a word. He walked down the alley to the street and then turned left.

He passed one man at the corner, but the streets were empty, no horses at the racks. A sliver of moon slid up over the darkened roof of a building across the way, and its silvery light took the ugliness from this rutted, frozen street.

Conway's lunchroom was on the next block, nearer to the railroad station, and on the opposite side of the street. The fact that Halloran was alone could mean many things. He may have met Clyde Morrison and had his talk, and now Morrison had gone out to the ranch. Or maybe Morrison had not even been on the westbound train, and Halloran was simply marking time here, trying to figure out what had become of the man he'd set out to kill.

Coming up opposite the lunchroom, Emmett stopped. Pulling back in the shadows under the wooden awning, Emmett loosened the gun in the holster and waited. Last night he'd been the hunted, but tonight he was the hunter, and he liked this role better.

Standing in the darkened doorway, he saw three riders go by in the street, their horses' hoofs ringing out on the frozen mud. As they swung through a patch of moonlight he recognized Curly Evans, Ben Adamson and Dave Howlett. Curly evidently had gone out to the line shack and learned from Ben Keefe that he was on Halloran's trail.

The three riders pulled up in front of the Longhorn, Curly dismounting hastily to look inside. They went on then to the Okay Livery to stable their horses, and Emmett decided he had to act before they came out.

Moving out into the road, he stopped there a dozen yards from the doorway of the lunchroom.

Taking the Colt from the holster, he pointed it up at the night sky and fired twice, the roar of the gun filling the quiet street.

Then he put the gun back into the holster and waited, knowing the shots would draw Halloran out into the open. He braced himself in the ruts of the road, legs spread a little, his right hand loose at his side.

There were a few moments of silence after the shots, and then doorways started to open all along the street. Saloon doors opened and men came out to investigate.

Emmett watched them out of the corners of his eyes. Curly Evans and the Pine Tree riders had run out of the alley of the Okay Livery. Then the lunchroom door opened, and Halloran's big frame filled the entrance. He took two steps out across the walk, and then stopped, seeing Emmett in the road but not recognizing him immediately.

Emmett called softly, "You know me, Halloran."

Then his right hand moved, because Halloran's gun was lifting from the holster. He heard Curly Evans yell, and he braced himself as he squeezed the trigger, shooting without haste.

He felt Halloran's slug touch the leather jacket on the right shoulder, and then he fired again, though he was sure that first shot had gone home.

Halloran started to walk straight toward him, the gun still in his hand, but he wasn't firing now. He walked forward like a man in a dream, coming out to the edge of the walk, and then he stopped, collapsing as if all the bones in his body had suddenly turned to water.

His body struck the frozen slush with a sickening thud, his hat falling from his head and rolling away. Emmett stood looking at him for a moment, and then he walked forward slowly. He could hear Curly Evans yelling his name.

Curly came up, panting.

"You all right, Emmett?" he puffed.

"All right," Emmett nodded. He holstered the gun and started to walk down the street toward the stable where he'd left his horse. Curly walked beside him as the crowd gathered around Halloran's body.

"Where to now?" Curly asked. "It's all over."

"Just beginning," Emmett Kane murmured. "You know if Morrison got in town?"

"Met him on the way out to Crown late this afternoon," Curly said. "I told him what's been happening out this way. He said Halloran offered to buy him out in town, but he turned him down."

Emmett thought of that as they turned into the livery stable alley. Halloran had known he was finished even before he died.

"Morrison went out to Pine Tree to see Madge Wilson about his stock in the valley," Curly was saying. "Reckon he'll fire that ornery crew Halloran hired, and start out fresh. Maybe he and Miss Wilson can get together now, since

Halloran ain't around to keep 'em stirred up."

Emmett was sure they'd get together. He said to Curly, "I'm heading out to Crown ranch."

"Seeing Clyde Morrison when he gets back?" Curly asked slyly.

Emmett smiled. "I don't have to see Morrison," he said.

Curly watched him as he led the horse out into the open. "Make it all right?" he asked.

"I'll make it," Emmett nodded.

"Luck," Curly said. . . .

It was past ten o'clock that night when Emmett rode down to Crown ranch. He dismounted in front of the house, and when he came up on the porch, stamping the snow from his boots, the door opened.

Pamela Morrison said to him, "I thought you'd be back quickly." She held the door open for him and he stepped inside, hat in hand. "It's all over?" she asked.

"All over," Emmett nodded. He noticed that her brother wasn't in the house, which meant that he was still at Pine Tree. He heard a clock ticking in the house.

"I suppose," Pamela said, "you had to kill him."

"No other way," Emmett told her. "He had his crew trying to kill me."

Pamela looked away from him as she stood by the open fireplace. "How is your wound?" she asked.

Emmett didn't answer the question. He said almost bluntly, "You like Wyoming, Pamela?"

"I love it," the English girl nodded.

"We'll see Texas first," Emmett said. "Then we'll come back—not here, but maybe near here."

She turned, smiling at him, and he could see the happiness in her dark eyes.

He stepped toward her, knowing that he'd made no mistake staying in this north country. It was a cold land, a land of long and rough winters, but it had its rewards for the man who could stick it out. The reward in his arms was sufficient for any man, rich and satisfying.

Center Point Large Print
600 Brooks Road / PO Box 1
Thorndike, ME 04986-0001 USA

(207) 568-3717

US & Canada:
1 800 929-9108
www.centerpointlargeprint.com